72nd & Rodeo

ALSO BY ROZ AVRETT —— *My Turn* ——

72nd & Rodeo

by Roz Avrett

ARBOR HOUSE ——— NEW YORK

Library of Congress Catalogue Card Number: 83-73063

ISBN: 0-87795-535-2

Manufactured in the United States of America
10 9 8 7 6 5 4 3 2 1

This book is printed on acid free paper. The paper in this book meets the guidelines for permanence and durability of the Committee on Production Guidelines for Book Longevity of the Council on Library Resources.

For the architect of Arbor House
and builder of writers—
Don Fine.

———

"You can forget about your Hong Kongs and your Arabs. You can shove your Swiss accounts. *I'll* tell you where the money is. It's right out there...on Rodeo Drive."

> Overheard at the pool, the
> Beverly Hills Hotel, January 1983

"The fashionable parts of the East Side are remarkably stable. (Since 1939), the geographic center has moved only slightly, to Seventy-second Street and Park Avenue."

> New introduction to *The WPA Guide to New York City*, 1982, William H. Whyte

ONE

New York City

"IT ISN'T *that* much further than the Hamptons." That's what Christy Shaw always said when people asked her why she weekended in Beverly Hills.

Monday through Friday, Christy was senior beauty editor at *Allure*, the magazine for today's dynamic woman. Saturdays and Sundays, she was wife to Tone Shaw at his stately pleasure dome on Rodeo Drive.

Everyone was fascinated by her bicoastal life. Wasn't it tiring? Didn't it put a strain on her marriage? What did she do for sex during the week? What did he do?

The commute was tiring. But Christy had learned to live with it.

As for putting a strain on their marriage, up until recently it seemed more that the week-long separations made things between them better. Tone was always so glad to see her on Saturday morning, kissing her and gushing the week's events as she half-listened in her jet-lag daze.

But without his charms—and even his most ardent detractors would admit they were considerable—Tone Shaw (he'd dropped "Anthony Grantland" the instant he'd adopted the neo-Italian West Coast cowboy look) was hell to live with. Christy found two days quite enough of his compulsive energy, incessant phone calls, and screechy playbacks from that damn tape recorder.

This morning he'd sounded particularly revved up, and it had been only six A.M. out there.

"Saturday's my fiftieth birthday, Chris. Remember? Good. Listen, bring Skeeter and Antonia. And tell those assholes at *Allure* you won't be back until Tuesday. So what if they don't like it? Tell them to shove it. Love you...." Clunk.

She'd stood still listening to the dial tone, wondering how the hell she was going to muster the energy to pack up Skeeter, Tone's impossible son from his previous marriage, and Antonia, his impossible daughter from their marriage. And wondering how much longer she could live like this.

A freezing blast of Manhattan wind slammed into Christy as she stepped from the shelter of the lobby of her building at 72nd Street and Park Avenue. She snuggled deeper into her down parka. It was the warmest thing she owned. Far warmer than the Blackglama mink she used only for client lunches. The parka was *her.* So were the pleated corduroys. Forget those chic little silk blouses and dresses with bows at the neck. So what if it raised eyebrows on the biddies at *Allure?*

It would be great to plunge into the pool with Tone, she had to admit. Even if he did keep it at 120°F. Christ, that was hot even for a hot tub, which in essence was what it was. A twenty-by-forty hot tub. But he wouldn't listen. He kept saying something about revitalizing the top layer of the epidermis.

Christy shivered and hugged herself. If anyone had told her that she would ever long to splash in the pool and stare lazily past the lemon trees into the hazy blue California sky, she would have looked at them and flatly said, "You're crazy." Everyone knew she was counting the minutes until the San Andreas fault opened up and sank California into the hungry Pacific. But here she was, freezing her ass off in what must have been ten below with the wind chill factor, dreaming about marinating in her husband's oversized bathtub on Rodeo Drive. And today she wouldn't have cared if Tone had an army of sycophants doggy-paddling in the shallow end.

Thank God she'd had the sense to call a cab. It was far too cold to watch sluggish Adolf the doorman stagger out into the traffic. At last her cab pulled up, its "on radio call" light flashing. A frozen couple tried to leap in with her. Any other day, she might have let them ride with her. But not today. She needed some time alone.

They inched around the corner. Lexington Avenue had developed arteriosclerosis. And she had developed a monumental headache. Must be nerves.

Double-parked cars, vans, delivery trucks, and busses traveling in packs, all conspiring to leave a single, narrow passage for traffic to trickle through—God, it was enough to make your life pass before your eyes.

She sighed and glanced at her watch. 9:38. The numbers were spelled out in Italian. She had another in French, and one in Spanish. Every year, she and Tone talked about going to Europe. In the end it was always the same: he could never spare the time. But Christy had learned the languages anyway and it had helped at *Allure,* so it wasn't a total loss.

They were stuck somewhere north of Bloomingdale's. Gridlock. She tried to relax. Shit. Why were women always *try*ing to do something instead of just doing it?

Why had she quit smoking? She didn't care what the

9

medical profession said—if quitting meant she was going to feel like the mother of *The Bride of Frankenstein* for the rest of her life, forget it.

Juneau Lamb would just have to wait—at the rate the cab was crawling she'd wait until the cows came home from Calcutta. Briefly Christy considered getting out and walking. Forget it. The sidewalks were as choked as the street and a hell of a lot colder.

What a day to hand in your resignation. But then, she'd done it plenty of times before. On glittering May mornings. Sweltering July afternoons. Hazy autumn evenings. And despite her awesome dedication to her *Psychology of Winning* cassettes, it always ended the same: Juneau Lamb, editor-in-chief, would talk her out of it.

Juneau refused to take Christy or her threats seriously. Again and again, she had poo-poohed Christy's reasons for wanting to leave. She had two weapons.

Her first was insulting Christy's intelligence.

"Only an idiot, Christy dear, a certifiable idiot would even consider leaving *Allure* to go with *Vogue* or Harpie's *Bazaar*."

Next she'd go to work on Christy's shaky financial status. Almost all the young editors at the magazine were heavily subsidized by rich parents. One father had joked about putting his daughter through *Vogue* after he put her through Vassar.

Christy had no parents, at least none that she knew about. She had been raised in a foster home. No trust funds to fall back on. Just her job, and of course, what Tone could contribute after his alimony check to the Great Bitch, Bette. Bette seemed to go through money like a rampaging brush fire. Christy sighed.

Whenever she thought about how much things cost, her mind wandered back to when she was a little girl, living with Aunt Vi and Uncle Harold, outside of Hingham, Massachusetts. How had they managed on

10

what they earned from their farm, dividends from their Sears stock and Aunt Vi's piano lessons?

Things *had* been cheaper then. Harold and Vi hadn't had a mortgage. They'd owned the farm free and clear. But Spirit had cost a lot. *Spirit.* Her wonderful, magical horse.

And of course Aunt Vi's colossal Buick, with fins and holes and a menacing chrome grille.

Both their sons had been killed in Korea. Two wholesome young men smiling eternally from the living room mantel. Vi and Harold practically never talked about them. Had the boys left their parents insurance? Now she wished she hadn't been afraid to ask Aunt Vi...about the boys, about her mother, about money. But now, it was too late.

On a rainy November night, Uncle Harold and Aunt Vi were coming back from the movies when their '52 Buick skidded and hit a giant oak.

Christy had answered the call herself, at the reception desk. The office manager had been very kind. Within the hour, she'd been on the shuttle to Boston. Two days later, she was back at *Allure*. She owned a farm, three hundred shares of Sears stock and a shopping bag full of photographs. She was eighteen years old.

Everyone at *Allure* thought the pretty receptionist was very brave. She had to be. She had no choice.

Now, at twenty-eight thou per year, Christy had topped the financial ladder at *Allure*. Without Tone and the apartment he'd inherited, she couldn't have existed in New York City much less lived, especially considering the expenses of providing general maintenance for Skeeter and Antonia.

Of course she could get a job in California but for half her salary at *Allure*. She figured she came out about $2,000 ahead. After plane tickets.

She knew when she married Tone that Skeeter was a

pain in the neck. But somehow, knowing *about* Skeeter and actually living with him in the same apartment were two very different things—kind of like the difference between hearing about kidney failure and actually getting it.

Talking to Skeeter on the phone and talking to him in his room was like talking to two different people. Writing letters to him about his clothes was easy; sitting in Brooks Brothers, watching him complain and squirm while the fitter pinned his shirtsleeves and trousers most definitely *wasn't.* Reading his accounts of hideous dinners with his bitch-mother was sort of fun. But he was Dr. Jekyll when they sat at the kitchen table, and Mr. Hyde when Christy took him to *La Bourgogne,* the beautiful and tolerant restaurant on East 72nd Street where, when Skeeter was being particularly unappealing, Jean-Claude would speak to Christy in French, his soft, caressing voice soothing away the cares of the day.

Allure. Manure, as Skeeter's best friend, Al Kurtz, called it. He could have a point. But Juneau would always say, "Listen to *Maman,* darling. Here at *Allure* you have financial security. Who *knows* what's waiting around the corner…in another job?" Her tone implying that job around the corner might as well have been as women's room attendant at the Port Authority Bus Terminal.

She had to face facts. She needed a larger salary. It was hard being so dependent on Tone.

Not that she wanted out. Or did she? But somehow the New York-L.A. commute which once added a feverish excitement to their weekends now just—well, just made her tired. What was happening to them? If only Tone would come to New York….

New York was so much more fun than Los Angeles, anyway. At least it used to be when they'd first met. She'd never known anyone like him—at *Allure* or anywhere else. He was nothing at all like the Mister No-wheres she seemed to attract from the woodwork.

She closed her eyes and remembered the night at Juneau Lamb's dinner party.

She'd been dreading it. She was always the youngest person in the room at these parties. Nineteen. And her clothes were—well, just okay. She always felt inferior. Inadequate.

And then something unexpected had happened the morning of the party: Juneau had given her a raise and a promotion. Christy was made a full-fledged assistant and Juneau expected her to dress the part.

"I want you to take the afternoon and go shopping, darling. Buy something spectacular for tonight. I'm having some very important people."

Juneau was always having some very important people, but Christy had been so happy about the raise and promotion, she flew out of the office and over to Saks.

When she'd appeared in a black velvet knicker suit with a red lace blouse, lace tights and satin pumps with cut steel buckles, Juneau had pronounced it "as chic as Araby," and introduced her to everyone as "my glitzy new aide-de-camp."

When Tone walked in the room his deep, dark brown eyes had immediately found her giant blue ones, and they'd just stared.

Juneau had seated them next to each other. They didn't speak to the people on either side and left almost immediately after coffee.

"Do you think you'd like a stinger?" Tone asked once they were outside.

"I think I'd love one." She'd never even heard of a stinger.

Tone had slipped his arm around her. "We were rude as hell, you know. Juneau will probably fire you in the morning if she doesn't call to fire you tonight."

"I don't think she will," Christy said slowly. Juneau had planned this. Other than the two married couples, they were the only straight people at the party. And she hadn't been too sure about one of those wives.

"I know how we can stop her, Christy."

"Stop her from what?"

"Firing you in the middle of the night."

"How?" she'd almost giggled. How naive did he think she was? Maybe she'd made a mistake and told him too much about life in Massachusetts with Aunt Vi and Uncle Harold. If *that* hadn't driven him away, nothing would.

"We can have our stingers at my apartment."

She'd really wanted to go to his apartment. He was thrilling. This was an adventure.

"As long as you promise not to show me your etchings," she'd said, laughing.

That had been that.

Tone's apartment, at 72nd Street and Park Avenue, was a wonderful, old, leather-and-oak rambling mess.

"I grew up here," he'd said. "I don't think the windows have seen new curtains since The New Deal. When the rugs got holes in them, my mother moved the furniture. If nothing else, it's made for some rather interesting groupings at parties."

By the time Tone had mixed the stingers, Christy was laughing so hard, her mascara had run into the corners of her mouth.

"Well, here's to your raise, your promotion and the rest of your life, Christy." He'd taken a sip and wrapped her in a kiss. She'd kissed him back. Their bodies strained together, her hips arching toward him. In a second, their drinks were forgotten and they were in his vast, old-fashioned bedroom, tearing off each other's clothes.

She didn't give a thought to the lace blouse that now

14

lay in a heap on top of the "chic as Araby" velvet suit.

She'd made love before a couple of times, but the others had been inept clods. Tone was delicious. He smelled wonderful. His body made her tingle.

He bit her ear lobes, kissed her eyelids and moved slowly down her neck with gentle kisses until he'd gotten to her hard, taut little breasts, her nipples coarse as gravel.

Her fingers found his penis.

"Christy," he groaned, "I think I'm going to explode."

"Me, too," she whispered, sliding under him and guiding him into her. There hadn't been time to move before they both came, his hot thunderous liquid spilling into her.

"Christy, Christy." He buried his face in her neck. He was damp, spent.

She'd never felt so perfect. It wouldn't last. It couldn't. Reality and happy endings had nothing to do with each other.

─────────────

She yawned just thinking about tomorrow. How was she going to get Skeeter on the plane? At least he *liked* her and Tone better than his mother, who only saw him when she wasn't at one of her precious international backgammon tournaments.

Skeeter was midway through the age of dumb. School was dumb. The weather was dumb. Their apartment was dumb. His father was dumb. And Beverly Hills was *really* dumb.

Last week Christy had told him that she refused to answer any questions or respond to any statements containing the word dumb.

Their conversation had since degenerated into curt nods and noncommittal "umms." Would she ever get through to him? Dragging him, sullen and hostile, to Tone's eternal party on Rodeo Drive certainly wasn't the answer.

That was tomorrow. Now, in a few more interminable minutes, she would glide across the marble-and-gilt lobby of the Centurion Building and up to the twentieth floor, home of the editorial offices of *Allure*.

Allure. The word stuck in her throat. Like the watercress sandwich with the headless roach she'd bitten into at Juneau's most recent command performance brunch.

This time she had to stick to her guns. If she let Juneau give her the "Listen to Maman" crap again, she'd kick herself. Pity the poor person who had Juneau Lamb for a mother. Funny, she'd heard Juneau did have a child somewhere. Christy ran her fingers through her black curls. Too bad Juneau had no sense of humor. She sure had a great sense of everything else. Lust. Greed. A need for control that would have made Catherine the Great blush.

Where was it written that women were the unknowing victims of unscrupulous men? Not in Juneau Lamb's book.

Christy drafted a mental scenario. Off with the parka and boots. Brush hair. Re-do makeup.

Check phone messages. Pick up coffee in its Spode cup with saucer. Shoulders high, march into Juneau's office.

Waving her toward the Chippendale wing chair with intricately carved hairy paws, Juneau would ask her to sit down. Christy would come to the point. No banalities about the weather. No explanations about being late. Explanations only got you into messes.

Juneau would pretend to listen. Calmly, graciously.

After a few minutes, she'd trot out the moth-eaten

16

scare lines. Prestige. Blah-blah-blah. Financial security. Blah-blah-blah.

When Christy remained adamant, Juneau would pick up the phone and dial Reed Doran, publisher of *Allure*, the only person she ever called directly. Reed would mumble something about taking Christy to lunch to Talk The Whole Thing Over. Christy would be dismissed with "Congratulations. Maman never lies."

But today would be different. She wasn't going to manipulate Juneau. Reed Doran was the only person who could do that. Or, maybe Reed Doran was the only person Juneau let manipulate her.

Anyway, Reed dictated the salary policy, and he felt that working at his brain child more than made up in prestige for what it lacked in take-home pay.

For nine years, Christy had bought his act. Until yesterday. Just before lunch, wages were frozen until further notice. The freeze had nothing to do with the state of the economy, losses in the publishing business, advertising revenues or anything else remotely intelligent. The offices of *Allure* were to undergo a facelift at the very expensive hands of Pumpkin Endicott-Osborne. And as anyone in Manhattan with a 10022 or 10021 zip code knew, she was the priciest decorator since Caracalla had raped the treasuries of the Roman Empire to build his fabled baths.

Christy had heard that it was going to take $3 million to do the reception room—that included statues and paintings. What the hell did they need with statues and paintings? *She* would have used the money to put some talent in the art department.

By closing time, rumors had ricocheted from the pink and silver walls. Reed must be having an affair with Pumpkin Osborne; Reed must be selling out to a conglomerate; Reed was divorcing Lane Reed and wanted to look poor, on paper, fast.

Some of the editors threatened to quit. Others wanted to hang on, get every nickel coming to them plus severance and unemployment.

No one really knew anything. Least of all Christy.

Juneau had summoned the editors to her office for champagne. Warm and short on bubbles, but champagne nonetheless.

"Darlings, Reed tells me that you can have everything in your offices. He says he's starting out with a clean sheet."

Someone sniggered.

"Take it home. *Allure* pays the moving bill. Re-do your flats, your weekend hideaways. Send it to auction. Get a tax deduction. It's all free as the air. Just one more of the perks here at *Allure*."

Juneau had Goddard-Townsend Newport antiques in her office, gifts from Reed over the years.

Christy had all-American French provincial worth a casual glance at a suburban garage sale.

Perks. Ha. There *had* been perks. Trips to exotic places with all the boring ladies from the other magazines, and all the gay caballeros from the advertising agencies and cosmetic companies. You could have more fun in the Christian Science Reading Room.

Last year, she had been to the Greek Islands to promote *The Golden Glow* for *Marquessa del Marca*. The year before, spring in Grasse to publicize *Fleur de Frolic Fragrances*. And of course there was *Roma Di Notte Romantics* shot in the Colosseum and *Traviata Camellia Complexions* done on stage at La Scala.

Glorious trips. If only Tone could have gone with her on just one of them. But he was always so damned tied up.

It hadn't always been that way. There was a time when he was never too busy to take her to a romantic little restaurant for lunch, never too busy to meet her at their apartment at noon and spend two hours making love before they'd gone back to their offices.

Then she'd had Antonia. When she'd been pregnant, sexy was the last thing she felt. She'd been depressed for months after, until she'd returned to *Allure*.

They had started to fall in love all over again, on a trip to Bermuda. Then Tone received word that he'd sold a song and they were on the next plane to L.A. Tone had rented a big Mercedes convertible from Budget-Rent-A-Car, and they'd torn around Beverly Hills like maniacs, eating, drinking, buying everything in sight.

One morning, as Christy had awakened, hung-over, in their bungalow at the Beverly Hills Hotel, she'd overheard Tone in the living room, talking on the telephone to a real estate broker. Talking about buying a house on Rodeo Drive.

He hadn't even mentioned it to her. She'd felt left out, betrayed.

She'd decided it was all part of his workaholic personality. She was a workaholic, too, but she wasn't nearly so impulsive. *She* thought things through. He just bulldozed ahead. You either went along with him, or you were left behind. And at the rate he went, you were left far behind, fast.

Two days later, they owned a pink house on the Drive, which Tone proceeded to gut and restore with pieces of old castles and mansions.

"You're always talking about the great perks at *Allure*, Christy. Well, this is one of the great perks for being Mrs. Tone Shaw."

Perks. At *Allure*. Nothing more than a euphemism for wooing and screwing between the worst possible combinations of people, all to sell the stuff of dreams.

"That's IT," Christy said out loud, *"Dream Street."*

It was the perfect name for the new line of cosmetics and fragrances from the enormous beauty conglomerate *Aromateria.*

Maybe it was too hokey, but *Dream Street* was loaded with hope. Just the thing Juneau and Reed would eat up. Or would they?

Trying to second guess Juneau was dumb, really dumb, as Skeeter would have said. What if they thought it was silly? Or course they wouldn't—hadn't *Moon Drops* done beautifully for Revlon? And what the hell were moon drops supposed to be? There wasn't a goddamn drop of moisture on the moon...

Suddenly, Christy was out of her funk.

Why did she always feel so worthless unless she came up with something new, something dazzling?

Her whole life, she'd been borne along by dreams. Her prayers were filled with "somedays"...her school days filled with promises to herself to be better, the best....

When she'd lived with Aunt Vi and Uncle Harold, she'd chosen good grades, winning trophies at local horse shows and hard work, over love.

The day she'd finally made it to Beauty Editor, beating out the North Shore Smith graduates, she'd decided to work even harder, moved by a dark fear that if she relaxed, she'd be fired, lose her identity...and Tone.

She'd tried to explain it to him one long evening over drinks. "I'm afraid I'll end up meandering in a bathrobe, not noticing if it's sunny or rainy, not caring if there's food in the fridge, because I'll forget to eat."

Tone hadn't understood.

"Don't be stupid, darling. You're describing someone who's lost touch with life."

How could she make him understand, that if she left *Allure,* it would mean exactly that?

On and on she'd driven herself, turning out more ideas in an afternoon than all of her editors together turned out in a week.

She'd even given Juneau ideas, rarely claiming anything for her own. It was beginning to depress her.

Her article, "The Last Word in Looking Good: Makeup Secrets from Forest Lawn," had started out as a smartass remark, developed into a story and upped single copy sales of *Allure* by thousands.

Juneau had taken all the credit. Reed had hinted that he knew who'd really done the article but he said nothing. Don't risk a mistress's wrath.

It was all Juneau's fault. Or was it? A part of Christy had always wanted to take care of her—but that part was getting smaller and smaller. She, Christy, deserved recognition, damnit.

Over and over again she'd wondered why her good feelings about herself depended so much on Christy Shaw, senior beauty editor at *Allure*—and not on Christy Shaw, wife and mother. She'd spent so much at her job that she no longer knew where it left off and she began.

Last week, Reed had told her that he wanted to use her picture in the promotional ads for the magazine.

"Christy, you personify *Allure*...the look of *Allure*. I want a close-up of you by that new photographer, Elizabeth. Posters. Newspaper ads. In-store displays. Whatever."

Her first reaction had been "I can't do that. Who'd want to look at me?" At parties, when the amateur photographers started snapping, she'd dash for the nearest bathroom. She was that skinny twelve-year-old again who never dreamed a man could ever fall in love with her. Even now when she looked in the mirror she didn't see the halo of blue-black curls, the giant, round dark blue eyes, the full, graceful mouth.

But Reed seemed to be genuinely excited about using her. And everyone said he had an instinct for talent. She had to trust his judgment.

When Juneau discovered that Christy was to portray *The Look of Allure,* she'd gone out to lunch, gotten drunk, and called Christy at the magazine from home.

"You conniving little wretch, the next thing I know, you'll be trying to get Reed into bed. I *know* you want my job." The phone had clattered to the floor. Christy could hear her sobbing.

Once everything had been fun. How had it all gotten so complicated?

The cab edged as close to the curb as it could without trapping its wheels in a foot of yellow-gray snow. $10.80. Plus tip. Just to go twenty blocks. She'd read in *The New York Times* that Manhattan cabs were among the lowest-priced in the country. Midas couldn't afford a cab in L.A. It was cheaper to rent a Rolls.

She pushed through the bronze doors of the Centurion Building. So what if Juneau decided she didn't like *Dream Street?* She was walking tall, shooting straight and getting the hell out of *Allure.* That would make Tone happy. She paused. But what about her? What would make her happy? Aunt Vi wouldn't have approved of her life. But then Aunt Vi had always known exactly what she wanted.

The Look of Allure. That would show them in Bell Glen High. It sure beat the class nerd showing up for reunion in the Cadillac with the blonde, both of them rented.

Even though Christy's loyalties were torn between Reed and Juneau, she always seemed to side with Juneau. Because Juneau was a woman? A vulnerable woman? It didn't really make sense. But somehow she knew it had to do with taking care of and being taken care of. Christy had always obeyed her blindly, until recently not even resenting it. Reed, on the other hand, treated her like a lady.

Maybe she owed him more? Like not making a scene, not making things worse than they were? And what would happen if she quit? She'd be doing exactly what Tone wanted her to do. She'd move to L.A. She'd lose her identity, that precious part of herself she'd been protecting so long she didn't even know if it made her happy anymore. How long could she go on being Juneau's slave and Tone's wet nurse?

God, it was too early to think like this. She'd think about *Dream Street.* It was good. A feather in her cap no matter where she went to work, even California. Now was not the time to get pessimistic.

———————————

As Christy walked toward her office, her secretary, Jamie Doran, was whispering into the phone. Gossip was Jamie's stock in trade. She also happened to be Reed Doran's niece.

There were no anti-nepotism rules at *Allure.* Quite the opposite. *Allure* was chockfull of relatives, friends, children of friends, and God knew, lovers of all conceivable persuasions and connections. It was as closely knit as an exclusive Long Island country club.

"Christy," Jamie said, looking very Cheshire, "Juneau would like you to join her for lunch at *Il Nido* on East 53rd Street at twelve-forty-five. Working lunch. Take something to write with. It seems that you've got to hire a new assistant. I've booked interviews for you throughout the afternoon."

Christy froze. What had happened to Tiffany Thomas? Had she been run over by a beer truck or something?

Only at *Allure* would one's secretary get the scoop first.

"Didn't Juneau reach you last night?" Jamie asked innocently.

No one had reached her last night. After a particularly nasty bout with Skeeter, she'd turned off the phones, put in ear plugs to blank out his TV and stereo and gone to sleep.

"No, Jamie, I was so tired I went to sleep early."

"Tant pis. Wait till you get the drift on this one. Ms. Thomas is going...are you ready, Madame...to work at *Aromateria*'s advertising agency. And for something new and different around here, a big raise. Ten thousand big ones more to be exact."

"Better come into my office, Jamie, and bring some coffee. Please."

"Now," she said, checking her reflection in her compact mirror as Jamie came in, "what is going on around here?"

"Last night, after you'd gone, Tiffany breezed into Juneau's office and gave two weeks notice. Just like that. Out of the blue, Juneau told her that she was a disloyal, sneaky, little cunt and to clear out of her office, get packing and screw two weeks, she had two minutes to move it. That's the whole story."

"Whew. That doesn't sound like Juneau," Christy lied. Juneau's language would have made Skeeter blush, but most people at *Allure* didn't know that. "Juneau hates dirty language. She doesn't even say 'damn.'"

"I know, I know. But Juneau was plenty upset. Not to leave this office, Christy," Jamie put her fingers to her lips, "but Juneau said Tiffany used *her* work to land the new job at the advertising agency."

That means Tiffany was using *my* stuff, Christy thought. That means she's getting ten thousand dollars more for *my* work.

"You may have noticed, Jamie, that ideas around here are about as valuable as used Kleenex." Let that get back to Juneau. Reed. Everybody. "Maybe I'd better call Tiffany."

"Not on company phones. I think—strictly *entre nous*—Reed is bugging them." Good old Jamie.

"Well, what about this afternoon? What's supposed to happen after my lunch with Juneau?"

"You've got several people to interview. Seven, to be exact. Resumes *ici*. Juneau chose six from the files. The seventh was a blind letter. I took it upon my humble self to set up an appointment for...him."

"Him? *Him* wants to be a beauty editor?"

"Him is Flemming Lord."

"Flemming Lord?"

"You know. The author."

"Never heard of him."

"Oh. Well, maybe you'd know him by his various noms de plume. Gloria Filbert. Janyce Chillingworth. Letitia van Buskirk. Now do you know who he is? Honestly, sometimes I wonder if you live in this century."

"What's he write? Gothic novels?"

"Come on, Chris, nobody writes Gothic novels any more. He writes romances. I mean, Chris, Flemming understands the meaning of life and love and sex and everything."

I'll bet. "Still, I've never heard of him but I guess I have to meet him since you've set up an appointment for me. Flemming von Buskirk?"

"Flemming *Lord*. Letitia van Buskirk."

"OK." She sighed. So far, today was like crossing Death Valley on her knees. "When?"

"Five-thirty. I thought we could, well, have cocktails or something in Juneau's office. Maybe I could take notes or something."

Jamie? Take notes? Jamie didn't do dictation, notes or windows. What the hell was going on here?

"Sounds like you've been busy while I was suffering in the middle of Lexington Avenue."

"I'll say." Jamie settled her silk tweed suited little body into Christy's heavily distressed fruitwood bergere. "Promise your lips are sealed, Christy, but I'd love to go to bed with this guy. I didn't think you'd mind."

Why should she mind? She'd never even met this...this person. What kind of a man wrote under women's names, anyway?

"Jamie, he's not hired. Chances are, he won't ever be hired. You know that."

"I know. I just want to meet him. Touch him."

Christy yawned. This Flemming character was already beginning to bore her.

"So tell me, Jamie. What else is new in this hotbed of the publishing industry?"

"You won't believe me."

"Try me."

"I've never been to bed with anyone."

This *was* shocking news. Jamie Reed, the bad seed, the wild oat. The former heartthrob of the Duke University campus. This sultry vamp, innocent as Antonia? Impossible.

For the first time in hours Christy laughed. "Well, maybe your maidenhead will be safe with Mr. Chillingworth. I wonder why he wants to work here?"

"Mr. *Lord,* Christy. Here's his letter. You'll flip." She held out a piece of stationery thick as cardboard and monogrammed with a crest. "He says he wants to expand his horizons. I hope to God he means it."

26

Two

Beverly Hills

"AND GOD said 'Let there be Miller Light,'" Tone Shaw announced as he climbed out of his overheated swimming pool and headed for his beloved deli fridge.

That fridge was a wizard. It chilled six hundred cans of beer at a clip. Not to mention various diet sodas, tonic, lemons, limes, olives, onions and the inevitable pitcher of fresh orange juice. All the ingredients of Life.

Christ, it was hot. Ten-thirty and almost 80°. Tone hated Celsius. Too confusing. He'd felt the same way about the new math. Where was the new math *now*? He couldn't name one person who liked Celsius, or even pretended to understand it. Except maybe Skeeter. That was the stupid, stubborn anti-social kind of thing that kid would claim to like just to be a pain in the ass. Celsius. Jesus.

He slid aside the glass door of the pool house and drank in the delicious cold for a minute before he reached for a beer. It felt good against his palms. Cool. Soothing. Maybe he *should* turn down the water temperature. Nothing drastic. Just ten degrees or so. Christy could be right about it being unhealthy. He'd asked his doctor, who'd muttered something about not believing in lingering death, but that sitting in hot water could make you impotent or infertile. So much for the medical profession.

He had to get his act together. He had a heavy day planned. First, to finish that article he'd started last night: "How to Win a Nobel Prize." Second, Jake Witt—a musician he'd discovered at the Universal Amphitheater— was coming to lunch to talk over Tone's newest song. And at three he had to teach his "Stairway to Stardom" course.

God, how it had galled him when Christy had refused to believe that anyone would pay fifty bucks a session for two lessons. Who cared if they'd all graduated from Yale Drama School?

He had to get a haircut. He had to have a workout. A massage. Even though he got up at six every day, there never seemed to be enough time for it all.

"Oh, rat fart." He'd forgotten his dinner date at The Bistro with Michele Quinton. As sure as his deli fridge would hum through the night, she'd wreck him for tomorrow. She was tireless.

He stretched and put the icy beer to his lips. Life was good. Not for one second did he regret giving up his phony baloney law practice in New York. Beverly Hills might not be the Athens of America, but it was him.

If only Christy would leave that moron magazine, get away from those jerks. Juneau Lamb. Reed Doran. Effete Eastern nincompoop names. Their real names were probably June Lard and Red Dork. He paused. Well, maybe those *were* their real names. But that was all that was real about them. Giggling over beauty secrets. Bullshit. Either you were born with it or you weren't. Plastic surgery could hike it up but fat asses, thunder thighs and Steinway stems were there to stay. Even reincarnation couldn't help.

He needed a cold shower.

If Christy would make up her mind to live with him he wouldn't need so many cold showers. And he wouldn't need the likes of Michele Quinton, either. He shuddered just thinking about that woman. He headed for the shower.

He scrutinized himself in the full-length mirror in the pool house dressing room. Five-eleven. Not tall but definitely not dwarflike either. Fighting weight. For fighting *what*? A little too tanned. No one had objected, let alone Michele, who maintained her skin a sort of light fruitwood. He looked closer at his chest. Damn. A couple of gray hairs. More than a couple bristling from his balls.

Graying at the temples might add an air of distinction, but the balls were bad news. He grabbed his solid gold tweezers from the red Florentine leather case and went to work.

"She loves me, she loves me not. She loves me, she loves me not." He was determined to extract every noisome gray hair if it took until lunch. So depressing. Growing old gracefully was a piece-of-shit philosophy. You couldn't hang out in your hot tub with grizzled pubic hair. He wasn't playing *Lear*.

Tone yawned. He was tired. Too many workouts. Too much dieting, jogging, swimming. Too much blaze of noon. He was beginning to look like Cochise.

He needed Christy. It always came back to that. More than just weekends. She was just about the only person he could really talk to. His shrink had told him not to try to force her to come out here for good. That it wouldn't be right for either of them. She was too headstrong for that. Headstrong was putting it mildly. She was about as flexible as anyone on Mt. Rushmore.

"You might need patience and understanding, Christy," Tone mumbled, "but so do I."

He thought about Skeeter. His own son had told him to his face that he was dumb. At the time he'd been livid but maybe the kid was right. Or maybe he should lay down the law. Christ, how was he going to do that? All he wanted was for Skeeter to love him, but Skeeter didn't seem to love anybody. Especially himself.

He stepped into the shower and reached for an oval, gold bar of *Tone* soap with cocoa butter. Not that he was a cocoa butter freak, he just liked to see his name in type. He started to sing:

> *Oh, life ain't so hard*
> *When you have a credit card.*
> *Who says you cain't charge*
> *Happ-i-ness?*

He'd been working on the credit card song for more than a week. Actually, Skeeter had inspired it when he told Tone all he wanted was free Mastercard for life. Christ. Kids.

Tone had been working with a basic Country feel. The only problem was he couldn't write music. All he needed from Jake was the feel. Jake Witt could make anything work. He was better than Beethoven.

"OK, Tone, take it from the top," he said to himself.

"OK, Jake," he answered, turning off the shower and reaching for a towel and his page of damp lyrics. He belted it out lustily:

> *The day you said you didn't care*
> *and took off with that millionaire,*
> *I charged to Wilshire Boulevard*
> *and got myself a credit card.*
>
> *I charged a condo at the beach*
> *and then I charged a Rolls Corniche.*

Cartier and Tiff-an-y—
Why they cain't git enough of me.

Charged a Piper Aztec plane.
Charged a case of French champagne.
Charged a custom-tailored suit
and they charged me through the snoot.

Now that I'm the credit king,
I can charge most anything.
Even a couple dozen beers
to help me through my useless tears.

I wish that my big spendin' spree
would bring you right back home to me.
But even though I miss you, honey,
I got the thrill of plastic money.

So ask me what I'm gonna do
when those big fat bills come rollin' through?
Why charge right to a telephone
and charge myself a big fat loan.

Oh, life ain't so hard when you got a plastic card.
Who says you cain't charge happ-i-ness?

"Bravo, Tone," Jake Witt shouted as he loped across the lawn. "I think you've got something there. I really mean it. It's your best work yet. A little more sentimental, maybe, but you're telling a good story. But more love, know what I mean?"

Tone was stunned. Was he actually hearing praise from Jake Witt? Jake had written the words and music for "Hug-a-Thon." If only Christy was here. She'd love "Plastic Money." Hadn't she always said credit cards ruined people's lives? He'd sing it for her tomorrow night at his birthday party, after he and Jake had had time to polish it. But what in hell did Jake mean, "More love interest"?

31

"Grab yourself a beer, Jake."

He couldn't wait until Christy arrived. It was always the same—whenever she walked in, he couldn't really believe she was *there*. To see him. He still couldn't believe she'd married him. Couldn't believe they had Antonia. Damn it. He knew he was hard to live with. He knew he drove her nuts. She drove him nuts, too. But he loved her. She was the loveliest woman he'd ever seen; ever gone to bed with.

Weekends were getting tougher. He'd always overwhelm her, trying to cram an impossible seven days into an even more impossible day-and-a-half. He dreaded Sunday mornings, eating breakfast and pretending to be happy, and trying to forget that soon she'd be gone for another eon.

Jake was walking toward Tone, a ridiculous grin on his face. He was weaving. Drunk? At eleven-thirty in the morning? How were they going to work on "Plastic Money?" Goddamnit all.

"How are they hangin', Tone baby?"

Why the hell did Jake always sound like such an asshole?

"Just let me make a call, Jake. Then we'll work."

He picked up his portable phone and punched Michele Quinton's preset number. He explained to her answering machine that he wasn't feeling well and would she mind if they postponed dinner? He'd see her tomorrow at his party. Click. He turned back to Jake and extended his hand. Jake did the same. An instant before they clasped, Jake lowered his hand to Tone's cock, damp and free under the towel, and grasped it firmly.

"Je-sus, Jake," Tone gasped.

"Like I always say, Tone, beauty is only foreskin deep."

Jake had to be high on something. His eyes were dilated. He dropped his hand from Tone's cock.

"Ah, Tone, come on. You and your heterosexual respectability. Who do you want to be? Batman or Robin? Holmes or Watson?"

Tone bolted for the safety of the pool house. Christ, all he'd ever wanted from Jake Witt was some good music for his lyrics.

Jake scampered after him, caught him around the waist and wrestled him to the grass. "What do you like about me, Tone?"

Tone writhed beneath him. "Your music, Jake. That's it. Now, come on. Get the hell off." Thank God no one was in the house, and his entire half acre was surrounded by an eight-foot-high hedge.

"My body, Tone. What do you like about my body?"

How had Jake gotten so strong? Even with all those workouts, Tone was no match for him—and the fact that Jake smelled like old, wet socks didn't help.

"I thought you were my *friend,* Tone."

"I *am* your friend, Jake. And I want to work on the song. Remember—the *song?*"

"I'll tell you what you should do, Tone."

"What?"

"Pick up a copy of *Gay American History.* It'll change your life, I promise."

Tone didn't want a copy of *Gay American History.* All he wanted was to get up off the grass and hear about how long it would take to bring the song to life and how much more it was going to cost.

"Maybe you should take a nap or something, Jake. Sleep it off, whatever it is."

Until now, it had always been some predatory women breathing into Tone's ears, especially after he'd divorced Bette, before he met Christy. This was too much. When, *if,* he told Christy, she'd probably laugh her head off.

"Tone? Tone? Where are you?"

The lyrical voice of Mirinda Felicia, his most promising acting student, tinkled in the steamy late-morning air.

He had to convince her to do something about that name. It was her fourth stab at a meaningful stage name. Never mind. She was here, and not a moment too soon. He pushed Jake away and struggled to his bare feet.

"Jake, hit the guest room until after I'm finished with my class. We'll work on the song later."

"You don't know what you're missing, Tone," Jake called out.

That's right, Tone thought. Thank God I don't.

"Twin jets. You'll never go back to coming and sleeping it off."

Twin jets? What the hell was that?

"Twin jets, Tone, is the ultimate togetherness. Simultaneous orgasm."

Mirinda moved around the hedge and into the garden. "Tone, I've just had a really, really great audition."

"Fabulous, Mirinda. Did you land something?"

"Not exactly. But lately, I've been getting turned down for bigger and better parts."

THREE

New York City

REED DORAN was worried about his prostate, his waist-line, and getting winded on the squash court. Most of all, he was worried about how he was going to end his long affair with Juneau Lamb.

It wasn't that he was tired of screwing around. Far from it. It was just that he was tired of her harangues. Somehow, his heart just wasn't in it any more. The last few times he'd met her at their Greenwich Village hide-away, he'd discovered that the old get up and go just wasn't getting up and going anywhere.

There was a time when he used to wake up at five in the morning, erect as a Maypole, anxious to get to the office, clear his calendar and tear downtown to the Hansel and Gretel cottage. Could anything bring back those days? Christ, he was only fifty-two. Was the Ghost of Christmas Future trying to tell him something? A shiver ran through him.

How could he get Juneau out of his life? It wasn't going to be easy. He didn't want to fire her. There was no reason to...no reason that the company would understand, anyway. He couldn't kiss her off in some chi-chi midtown restaurant where she'd be afraid to make a scene. He'd loved her too long and too well for anything that sleazy. He loved her now, damnit all.

Why hadn't he gotten a divorce and married her years ago when they were like a pair of rutting hogs, each other's scent wild and randy in their nostrils?

He'd given her the best years of his life. And she him. If the truth were known, they'd both given the best years of their lives to *Allure*.

Why did he feel so empty? He'd been good to her. Damn good. He'd made her the highest-paid magazine editor in New York. Maybe anywhere. Not to mention the Newport antiques he'd bought through the company. He couldn't let her keep them, but at least he'd given them to her. Lane didn't know about them but even if she did, she wouldn't care. All his wife cared about was her girl friends.

When it came down to it, the trouble between them was the magazine. If only Juneau hadn't been so boring and demanding about it. Lately, it seemed that she loved it more than him. Was that why he'd jumped into bed with Pumpkin Endicott-Osborne? Well, that's what he'd told himself, anyway.

God, what a body that woman had. Tough. Lean. Everything he thought he didn't like until he'd tried it. No wonder he'd signed a contract with her to do over the offices at *Allure*. With all Juneau knew about diet, exercise, health and beauty, she couldn't compare with Pumpkin.

Why did life have to be so complicated? Ah, for the good old days. A man, a plan, a canal.

Eleven-thirty. He'd have to leave in ten minutes if he was going to make it to the Village on time. And he had to be on time—he wasn't up to Juneau's wrath this morning. Mrs. Osborne had kept him up most of the night dancing, drinking, fucking, laughing. An army of red ants was marching through his stomach.

What a fool he'd been. A nine-year affair. No one had a nine-year affair.

But Juneau had never mentioned getting married. He'd have to give her that. There had been no tearful demands to divorce Lane. Juneau was a lady. She knew how to behave. And at his age, he liked ladies. He didn't want to hear about equality. Women's Lib. All that shit. He liked ladies in silk dresses and Chanel suits, in dark stockings with seams and four-inch heels.

A small, sharp pain shot through him. Just the idea of the prostate operation made him tremble. It wasn't supposed to affect your sex life, but you weren't *supposed* to contract diseases from toilet seats, either.

Face it, sport, you're not getting any younger. And neither is Juneau. Maybe it was his imagination but she seemed to have been putting on weight lately. Bloat from all those martinis, the elixir of the cosmetic and beauty book set.

Christ, how could he have spent his life with these nincompoops? A graduate of Northwestern. A starry-eyed serious young journalist who'd evolved into...into what? A functioning alcoholic, married to a functioning lesbian at night and a functioning pile of coated stock glitz during the day.

Reed pushed the intercom button. "Take messages, Miss Scott. I'm going to the Racquet Club."

"But I neglected to book a squash game, Mr. Doran," the British clip replied.

"Actually, Miss Scott, I am going to the doctor but I do not want that information tripping over the inter-office telephone wires. Just a check-up."

"Very good, sir."

"Back by three, Miss Scott."

Juneau Lamb paced the tiny living room of their cottage. It was the perfect *Back Street* setting, smack in the middle of a hidden garden behind a pair of brownstones on West 12th Street.

She'd spent so many lazy, lovely hours here with Reed over the years. But an odd chill had come over her in the cab. The storm, maybe. Her nose was running her eyes were watering. But it was more than just the weather. It was Reed. He'd been so cool lately.

And things had been going well at *Allure*. Until yesterday, that is, when Tiffany Thomas had left for that ditsy advertising agency.

Why had she made a lunch date with Christy Shaw anyway? Christy could hire a new assistant on her own. But she was always threatening to leave and with Tiff gone, now would be the opportune time for her to strike again. Christy couldn't leave. She was as important to Juneau's career as Reed Doran.

For almost nine years, she had advised her, edited her, and now she was so dependent on Christy that she was almost afraid to make a move without consulting her. No one knew—especially not Reed.

If Christy walked, Juneau wouldn't be able to replace her fast enough to cover her tracks. Or maybe she'd never be able to replace her...she'd have to do her own work; deal with Reed's discovery that she was a no-talent. Christ. She'd be out in less than a month. And out was no place for a forty-four-year-old, overpaid magazine editor—a pregnant forty-four-year-old, overpaid magazine editor.

Juneau lowered herself into one of the overstuffed Thurber easy chairs that flanked the fireplace. She struck a match. In a moment, the fire was more alive than she.

———————————————

Reed was going to miss the silly little cottage. It brought back memories of a horny college kid, sneaking off for the weekend. It was much more of a home than either his Fifth Avenue octoplex or his beach house in East Hampton.

Maybe he could find a new occupant? Forget it—not even Pumpkin Endicott-Osborne. She'd redecorate it in High Tech or High Episcopal and spoil everything.

Maybe Christy Shaw...he'd been thinking about her for ages. Great body. Mischief in her eyes. Clever. Probably liked popping corn *and* champagne corks. He'd wanted to screw her the first time he met her. Too dangerous, though. Then. And now. He had only one place to hide from his open-book life, and it was already inhabited by a tigress—a jealous one at that.

He turned his key in the familiar lock and stepped in out of the snow. A fire. Good. Juneau was sitting, as always, next to the fireplace. She seemed happy to see him.

"Reed, darling, too early for a bloody?"

He walked over and kissed her.

"Somewhere in the world they're having cocktails." Christ, even their banter was edging into senility.

Automatically, he reached under her skirt and cupped her ass in his hands. *It* certainly wasn't putting on weight.

"How are you, babe?" He pulled her up and kissed her again. His penis began to leap. She smelled wonderful. Maybe something could happen....

As long as she didn't start talking about the magazine. Just for twenty minutes. That's all he needed.

"The inventors of pantyhose should be drawn and quartered," he whispered. "Say something nice and dirty, darling. You know how much I love your filthy mouth."

He kissed her neck, her arms, her breasts.

"I know *where* you love my filthy mouth, Reed." For

a famous publisher, he certainly had a strange view of the English language.

She undid his belt and unzipped his trousers. A second later, he was naked from his waist to his ankles, with her tongue darting along the taut underside of his jutting prick. Ecstasy. Reed sighed.

He was nuts. Definitely. But Juneau had always been able to get it off the ground. Lane couldn't; hadn't even tried since the early Seventies. Maybe earlier. None of his nasty nooners could either. No matter who he was with, even the glorious Pumpkin Osborne, his thoughts always came back to Juneau. She was a part of him.

He scooped her up and carried her into the square little bedroom. It was warm and intimate, but the sheets were mercilessly cold and smelled of mildew.

Their lovemaking exhausted them both. Reed had started out tired, and now he was whipped. Juneau lay on her back, an arm flung across her eyes. But Reed could tell she'd been crying.

Oh, Christ, here it comes. Give Christy a raise. Why didn't he just give Christy Juneau's job? She'd been doing it for years. And Juneau thought no one knew. What a joke. It was his fault. He'd protected her. Where would Juneau have gone if he hadn't fallen in love with her? Where would she go now?

"Do we have to talk about the magazine? Just this once, couldn't we discuss something interesting?"

"It's not the magazine, Reed. It's something else. Something well...more important."

Something more important than her beloved *Allure*?

"I'm not so sure how you're going to take this...that's why I've been putting it off."

Great. Maybe she was going to retire, let Christy move up. Then she'd make more demands on him than ever.

"I'm pregnant." The words bit into her heart. She'd

said them once before, twenty-seven years ago, to someone quite unlike Reed Doran.

––––––––––––––––––

It had been at the end of the most romantic summer of
her life. Even now, on lonely nights, on solitary walks
home from the office, she still thought of him. The
blond Yale student in his silver Jaguar who could have
had any girl and did, but not before he'd had the beautiful, impressionable townie, Jane Conroy.

Would Ian Harrington, only son of the house-on-the-
hill-Harringtons, recognize her today?

For years after he had vanished, she still looked for
him—in restaurants, museums, Central Park, her breath
catching every time she saw a tall blond man.

But if she found him, what would she have said? What
would he have said? The last time she'd spoken to him
had been that night she told him she was pregnant. He'd
promised to send her some money. That was all. Later,
she'd received a check for $10,000 from a Rose-Delia
Harrington, in Palm Beach. She'd spent the summer
with a childless couple, had the baby, and left her with
them, along with the money.

Well, there was nothing Reed could say to make her
give this child away. Anyway, she knew he'd always
wanted a son, even if he'd never said so.

––––––––––––––––––

He lifted his face from her shoulder, with a look she
couldn't quite read.

"But you can't be pregnant, Juneau. You're forty-six."
Pregnant. All these years he'd never told her how much
he wanted this.

"Forty-*four*, Reed. And I am most definitely pregnant.
Please spare me the indignity of asking whose it is."

41

"I think, my darling, you'd better cancel your lunch date with Christy," Reed said gently. "We have a lot to discuss. But first, I'm going to open a bottle of champagne."

"I don't know why I made a lunch date today, Reed. I guess, well, I thought you might...be:...mad...at me."

"You knew damn well I wouldn't be mad at you. Mad hardly expresses how I feel. I'm well, bowled over, I guess. This is a first for me, you know."

"I didn't know. Maybe I guessed. I never understood why you and Lane didn't...don't...I could never bring myself to ask...."

Reed folded her in his arms. "This may be the happiest day of my life. I'm sorry I don't have any fancier words to express it. But it's simply that: the happiest day."

"I've had such mixed feelings, Reed. It's quite a revelation, you know, to discover something so momentous so late in the day." If only this had happened thirty years ago, how different her life might have been. She'd searched for the child, even hired the lawyer Tone Shaw, when he'd lived in New York, to trace her. But nothing had ever come of it. It was as though the child had never existed.

"Juneau, there's something you don't know. I have to have an operation."

"Operation? What kind of an operation?" Please, God, don't let him say cancer, she prayed.

"It's a man's operation. Prostate. Guess I'm that age." He paused. "It's not serious. Don't look so stricken, my darling."

"Oh, I know, Reed. We ran an article on it a couple of issues back, remember?"

"I didn't read it. On purpose." How could any woman understand what prostate surgery meant? The threat of

42

castration. Sterility. Sharp knives slashing around down *there*. He shivered. He was tired. He was terrified. Suppose he could never get it up again after the operation? The news about the baby couldn't have come at a better time.

The doctors had explained that his fear was normal. That almost everyone felt the same way. But who gave a shit about *every*one? The doctors sure as hell didn't. Slice it out. Sew it up. Collect $2 million. Do not go to jail. Or even to court for malpractice.

"Oh, darling," Juneau laughed, "what a day we're having."

"Juneau, do you think the baby will be OK?"

"I'm a little old for a first baby, but I've had all the tests. I'm terribly healthy. Like the proverbial horse."

"Does anyone else know?"

"My doctor. The lab people, who couldn't care less. And now, you."

"What do you think we should do?"

Was he hinting that she should get an abortion? Juneau bit her lip. Let him talk. She'd been handling him like that for years.

But what she didn't know—couldn't know—was that Reed Doran hadn't been so moved, so unnerved, since he'd accidentally set the dining room draperies on fire. Instead of taking a ruler to his bare behind, his mother had shocked him by bursting into tears, relieved that he hadn't burned himself. Never mind the antique velvet draperies from Paris.

Reed had no children. Lane had never wanted to bother. She'd been too busy living life, as she'd said many times. She'd rarely created opportunities for love-making and so Reed had married *Allure* and gradually drifted into an affair with Juneau. A year into the affair, they'd fallen in love.

Now it all seemed clear. Juneau was his true wife. The only woman he had ever loved. Nooners and weekend pick-ups at cocktail parties didn't count. *How* could he have been such a horse's ass? He couldn't live without her for twenty-four hours. How could he even have thought of exiling her? Here she was, about to give him everything he'd ever wanted...and he had never been able to tell her. A child would make his empty, silly half-over life. Hell, his life was more than half-over, unless he made it to one-hundred-four. Which at this rate was highly unlikely.

"Juneau, did we ever discuss children?"

Christ, what was he up to? "I don't think the subject ever came up."

"Are you positive that I never hinted that I might divorce Lane if you and I could have one?"

"Well, maybe once or twice. But that was ages ago." Reed laughed.

"Here's our chance to give the biddies and pansies something to dish about. A regular gourmet casserole."

Juneau stiffened. How could he think that way?

"Do you think I could take that?"

"It's just that I thought...well, it never occurred to me that you'd want to stay on at the magazine. You know better than I that Christy Shaw can take over."

He *knew*. How long had he known?

"I'm not sure, Reed. You know how much *Allure* means to me." Did it mean more than Reed? They were interchangeable.

Reed hugged her. She could have an abortion. Lane could go on doing her living. He could go on screwing around and meeting Juneau whenever. She would have gotten an abortion if she'd wanted one. She didn't want one.

But a child was a big decision. Especially at his—*their*

ages. It would change his life in a big way. Maybe for the better. So many of his friends had dumped their buffalo-mama wives and married younger women. They were having babies left and right. The old goats claimed they'd never been happier. He glanced down at Juneau cuddled beside him, her eyes wide. She was magnificent. He kissed her.

"Well, babe, what do you think?"

"Think?"

"Do you want to go through with it? Get married? Chuck *Allure*? We can find someplace to live. There's a great house on Beekman. Not cheap. We've got a head start on the furniture with all the stuff in our offices."

"Married?" Juneau's voice shook. What was wrong with her? She'd wanted to marry Reed for eight years. It wasn't exactly an anti-climax. Not exactly.

Shit, Reed thought, I haven't been flowery enough. But then he'd been plenty flowery with Lane and look where it had gotten him. He pulled Juneau closer.

"I want you to be my wife, Juneau. I've wanted it for such a long time. You're not afraid, are you? It's not as though you were facing the great unknown."

When weren't you facing the great unknown? "Oh, Reed. Yes. Yes. Yes."

"Juneau, I want to talk to you seriously...about these tests. Maybe I should talk to your doctor."

"You don't believe I'm pregnant. Is that it?"

"That's not it at all. I'm worried about you. I want to know the risks. Everything. I'm involved, too, you know."

"I told you that the risks were minimal. It's much, much riskier with a first child." She paused. It was time to tell him. "This isn't my first, Reed." There. She'd said it.

Reed held her close and stared at the wall behind her soft, blonde hair. Juneau had never mentioned a child.

Or a husband. Who, where was the child? But now wasn't the time to ask.

Damn Pumpkin. Damn Lane. Damn *Allure*. Damn everything. Reed Doran, lawyer, lover, publishing magnate, was about to become a father. To produce an heir to his publishing empire. He felt like shouting, sending telegrams. But first he had to get a divorce.

The snow had started again, much harder than yesterday. It hissed down the chimney and into the fire.

If they stayed in the cottage much longer, they weren't going to be able to get back to the magazine until late. Maybe not until tomorrow, depending on the snow plows.

"Reed, I have to call Christy. She's probably waiting for me at *Il Nido*."

"I'll leave a message at the restaurant."

"What about *Allure*? Those meetings this afternoon?"

"I've just decided. I'm closing the office. Snow alert," he laughed. "After all, *we're* marooned, why should all my valued employees have to bed down at the office?"

The phone rang in the living room and Juneau jumped.

"Who knows we're here?"

"No one. You and I are the only ones who know the number."

"Someone else must, love," Juneau murmured into his ear.

"It's a wrong number." Couldn't Pumpkin somehow have discovered the number? Impossible. It was unlisted. He continued to kiss Juneau's breasts. Her flesh was the flesh of an Ingres painting. Ivory silk subtly flushed with palest pink.

"Maybe I should make those calls," Juneau said.

"First things first." Reed pulled down the covers and gently spread Juneau's legs. He drew her to the edge of the bed, tracing the inside of her thighs with his tongue. He closed his eyes.

46

Pumpkin would have had his neck locked in the vice of her muscular legs. She would have been making eerie, primordial noises, more like a trumpeter swan than a woman in the throes of passion.

There was something to be said for Juneau's passivity. How she could be so defiant at the office and so lethargic in bed had always puzzled and intrigued him.

He knelt in front of Juneau's open thighs and moved slowly, determinedly forward. Just before he was about to penetrate, he stopped, his erection faltering. The child was in there. What if he did something to hurt it? Juneau's body had become something holy. Slowly he moved away.

"Reed? Are you all right?"

Must be his damn prostate getting to him. Never once in nine years of thorough, driving stars-in-the-sky sex had he ever lost an erection.

She grabbed the ice cubes from her Bloody Mary and thrust them under his balls. He jerked backward.

"I'd forgotten about that," he moaned.

"The iceman cometh, as they say," she laughed.

"This iceman is going to put on some clothes, open some champagne and find us some lunch."

FOUR

New York City

"Do you think Jesus is watching you?" Ed Kurtz asked
Skeeter Shaw. He blinked his eyes, trying to see through
the fog of pot smoke. His mouth was full of pizza, some
of which had dribbled on Christy's eggshell moire sofa.

"Probably not," Skeeter answered without much conviction.

"Who do you think is?"

"Is what?" Skeeter's conversational abilities were beginning to flag. His motor coordination wasn't much
better.

"Is watching you?"

"Ed, you are dumb."

"I wish you'd stop calling everyone dumb. No one is
as dumb as you say they are."

"How do you know?" Skeeter took a long draw and
held it in.

"Because *no*fuckingbody is *that* dumb. You're into overkill, Skeets. Everything to the tenth power."

"Don't call me Skeets. Sounds like some kind of dumb
disease. 'Hello, Mrs. Kurtz? This is Doctor Dong. It seems
like your son, Edmund Kaiser Kurtz, is suffering from
an advanced case of Skeets. Yes, it *is* a rare disease. We

haven't seen too many cases lately. No, definitely *not* fatal, Mrs. K., but sometimes the victim would be better off if it were.'"

Howling, Skeeter and Ed rolled over on the living room carpet, splashing red wine and pizza.

Ed leaned against the sofa. Tears cut paths through the dirt on his face. "Christ, Skeets, you oughtta go out to Bev Hills, move in with your old man, and become a famous Hollywood screen writer. Or a comic. Or *something*. You could put Richard Pryor out of business... You still didn't answer my question."

"What question?"

He was hazily aware of the state of the living room. His ass was going to be in hot water. But Christy never got off his case anyway so what was another load on his back? He rose unsteadily, accidentally kicking the wine bottle. The carpet slurped up the last drops. He giggled. Maybe if he opened the rest of the case they could have a red carpet. He squinted. Was that his buddy Ed Kurtz across the room?

"What profound question am I supposed to have ignored, Edmund Kaiser Kurtz?" He lurched into a pink velvet chair and knocked it on its side.

"Who do you think is watching you? That is, if you don't think Jesus is watching you?"

"What is this Jesus stuff? Why should Jesus watch *me*? He's got lots more interesting people to watch than me. I mean, he could watch the traffic jams on the Long Island Expressway. Or Margaret Thatcher. Or things in orbit. Or dogs humping in Central Park. Just because I'm not Jewish, you have this dumb—that's right, dumb thing in your head that I go around all day thinking Jesus is watching me. There's a name for that, Ed. Paranoia. Know what I mean?"

"People aren't supposed to be paranoid unless they're

extremely bright and over thirty," Ed said smugly. He inhaled.

"Well, do you think this Jesus stuff is? I mean, do you think I'm a Jesus freak or something? And while we're at it, Ed, what kind of freak are *you*? Besides a dumb freak?"

"OK, I'll tell you," Ed whispered. "The kind of freak who wants everything his parents have without going through all the shit *they* went through to get it. If that makes me a freak, hello, Barnum and Bailey."

"You've got a point, Ed. I wouldn't exactly mind that. Just a check once a month. For a nominal amount."

"But it doesn't happen that way, Skeets. You have to work for it."

"My mother doesn't work for anything."

"Christy busts her behind down there at *Manure*. She's a biggie. My mom reads everything she writes."

"Better not let her hear you call it *Manure*, Edmundo. And besides, Christy is *not* my mother. She's Antonia's mother. Bette Farmington, never-pay-for-anything queen of the backgammon tournaments, is *my* mother. Antonia isn't as screwed up as me because she's not the product of a divorce. See?"

"Do you call her Mom, Skeets?"

"I call her dumb."

"She doesn't sound so dumb to me."

"Look what she did to Dad and me. That was real dumb."

"Like what? Moving to Palm Springs and playing backgammon twenty-four hours a day? Doesn't sound too bad."

"How would you like it if your mother never spoke to you?"

"I'd like it. I'd like it."

"Bullshit."

51

"My ears would stop ringing. They're ringing right now."

"Ed, it's the phone. One of us had better answer it."

"Well, Skeets, it's your phone. *You* better answer it."

"But you don't sound as whacked as I do."

Skeeter heard Antonia pick up the phone on the fourth ring. Little sneak had probably been listening to their conversation. She kept her back to them, said a few words and hung up.

"Antonia, what's up?"

Antonia stood in the arch between the foyer and the living room. She wanted to laugh but the sofa, carpet, wine and pizza were getting less funny by the minute.

"Skeeter, we've got to get some salt and club soda and get the wine out of the rug. And the sofa. Mother will have a fit. And for once, beloved Skeets, I'm on *her* side. What have you men been doing, anyhow?"

"Nothin' beats some pot 'n pizza." Ed rolled his eyes, patted his head and rubbed his stomach.

"You should be packing, Skeeter. Tomorrow, it's big bird time to the Coast."

"Five billion Kopeks says that no dumb big birds are taking off for the Coast or any other place. You *did* notice the precipitation? That's snow, in case you're not conversant with the word," Skeeter said smugly.

"Precipitation can be snow, rain or sleet," Antonia snapped. "Now, who's getting the salt and club soda before this wine really sinks in?"

Ed looked up.

"How about *Visine*? It gets the red out. Ten zillion-trillion gallons of *Visine* to the rescue."

Antonia ignored him.

"While you disgusting persons are cleaning up, I'm going to pack for California. You *do* know it's Daddy's

52

birthday tomorrow, don't you, Skeeter? I'll bet you never even got him a birthday present. I suppose I'll have to do it for you, imbecile."

"Cool it. Of course I bought Tone a gift. Why do you always think I don't do what I'm supposed to, huh?" He smiled. There were bits of anchovy sticking to his chin.

"Well, then you'll make *The Guiness Book* under Amazing Firsts," she said sourly.

"Ed," Skeeter commanded, "get salt and soda and fix up this mess. I'm going to shower."

"If this room isn't perfect by the time I'm finished packing, you guys are going to be in hot water. *Scalding.* My mother can be very tough, Ed." Antonia marched from the room flipping her blue-black hair like an impatient filly. "And I'm not just kidding," she called back over her pink cashmere sweater.

Ed and Skeeter struggled to their feet, clutching at each other. The room spun. They giggled. They couldn't seem to stop giggling. Never had anything been so funny. What in particular? Everything.

"Hey, Ed, can you see?"

"See what? I don't have X-ray vision."

"X-rated vision." They collapsed again.

"Outside. Look out the window." The windows swam in and out of focus.

They inched across the room to the big triple windows overlooking Park Avenue. Fourteen stories down in the snowy silence, the traffic lights turned from misty green to misty red to misty green. Nothing was moving in the street. The ghostly outlines of parked cars had almost disappeared in the white on white.

"What makes the lights look so funny?"

"I don't think those lights are funny. Not as funny as your sister. 'My mother is very tough.' Ha-ha."

53

"I mean all fuzzy," Skeeter groaned.

"That's snow, dunderhead. Snow. You've heard of it? Very big in Alaska, I'm told."

"It sure is quiet."

Just the whirl of the wind and the hiss of the snow against the glass. The drifts on the panes were almost two inches high.

"Nature is having a ball, Skeeter, and we didn't even notice. Let's go outside and make a snowman."

"You've got to be dumb, Ed. Who do you think you are? Fucking Admiral Byrd? This is supposed to be the biggest snowstorm since '47 or '61 or '78. I can't remember. We can't go out there. People are going to start dying from exposure. We're not going anywhere. Except to the kitchen. We've gotta get rid of this mess."

"You'll never die from exposure, Skeets. You might be arrested for indecent exposure, though." Neither of them laughed. The effects of the pot were wearing off.

"I'll tell you who's the dumbest of all, Ed," Skeeter said, his eyes dark. "Christy and Tone."

"How can you call your parents...excuse me...your dad and stepmother, by their first names? Why don't you call them Mom and Dad?"

"They don't call me Son."

"That's different," Ed replied, picking up the bottle and sucking out the last drops of Chateau Mouton Rothschild '61. He scooped up the square, white cardboard box holding a last sodden red-and-green triangle. "Old anchovies stink," he pronounced. "You know?"

"Christy and Tone...my Dad and stepmother are *dumb*. They're crazy about each other. Bonkers. But she lives here and he lives there."

"Maybe he can't stand you and Antonia."

"That's not true."

"Why do they commute all the time, then? I mean, people bitch about taking the train from Scarsdale or

Westport. How can your stepmother handle the old red eye from L.A.?"

"Beats me. You should try it. Hey, why don't you fly out with us for Tone's birthday?"

Ed, who lived two floors below the Shaws with his widowed mother and her impossible lover, considered it. Better than the Hamptons. Or Atlantic City. He'd love to hop on a 747, order a drink, watch a movie.

"Can I really?"

"Can you really what?"

"Really go to L.A.? Wow. You'd think it was *my* birthday." Ed danced around the room, and careened into a black lacquer Regency chair.

"Hope your old lady isn't overdrawn at the bank, Mr. Kaiser Kurtz. That's the world's most expensive firewood. Hand-painted by blind monks in Malaga. Got the picture?"

"Oh." Ed sank to the floor. "We should've gone out and made that snowman."

Antonia reappeared.

"Mother will be back any minute, guys, and if I were you, I'd be scared."

Skeeter rolled his eyes.

"We're trying. We're trying. Ed has done a great job on the rug. It looks better already."

"It looked a lot better before lunch," Ed observed.

Doctor Watson, Skeeter's boa constrictor, slithered out from under the sofa, straight over to the box containing the last wedge of anchovy pizza, and swallowed it whole.

Ed grimaced.

"Boas don't eat pizza."

"It's Doctor Watson's second favorite."

"I'm afraid to ask...what's his first?"

"A rat. Nice. Big. Juicy. I gave him one yesterday so he wouldn't be hungry on the plane."

"Rat? How do you fix—cook—a rat?"

"What do you think, stupid? You put it in the toaster-oven." The reality of the situation was beginning to dawn on Skeeter. The living room was an unholy mess. They'd demolished two bottles of beyond-the-dreams-of-avarice expensive wine. Two zillion dollars worth permanently absorbed into the carpet and sofa. "This is not a pretty sight, Edmund Kaiser Kurtz," he said thoughtfully.

He wasn't packed. He hadn't gotten his father a birthday present. And that was the good news; he'd flunked his English exam this morning.

No one had ever flunked an exam at The Tutoring School. It was impossible. The largest class was one teacher to four students; the smallest, one teacher to two. English had been three-to-two. Once again, Skeeter had truly distinguished himself.

Christy would ask for an explanation. What could he tell her? What could he tell Tone after he'd practiced on Christy?

Maybe he should tell the truth. He'd been at The Museum of Natural History, checking out the snakes. He loved snakes. He didn't love Shakespeare, although he had to admit that Will was the best of the worst.

He lurched to his feet, picked up the pizza box, an empty wine bottle, and walked, almost steadily, to the kitchen.

Somehow he knew it was going to be a long night and an even longer weekend.

FIVE

New York City

CHRISTY SIFTED through the papers on her desk.

The Wife of Bath medieval bath line was going full steam ahead and would be introduced at the Roman baths in Bath, England, in June. Typical. Just as she was about to resign, along came a glamorous trip.

Skeeter would love to go. So would Antonia. They hated all Christy's trips, or at least that's what they said. Maybe they really did want to go. She'd been selfish about not taking them—but the idea of two teenagers thrown into the nest of *Allure* editors and beauty product manufacturers was just too much.

Oh, the hell with it. She'd wait until after Bath to quit. She'd pack up Tone and the kids. Hand them their plane tickets. That way, they couldn't back out without a fuss. Who was she kidding? Since when had that ever stopped them?

The phone rang. It was Tone, asking her to listen to the tape of a new song he'd written, something about plastic money. He sounded the way he used to sound before their relationship had begun to melt. But something was wrong. She could hear it in his voice. Beyond the exhilaration. For some reason, he had decided not to work with his new arranger. God, it wasn't easy to keep things in perspective from 3,000 miles.

"The song's great. Who's going to do it?"

"Not sure. When can you and the kids get here?"

"There's a blizzard here. Haven't you heard the news?"

"No. No blizzard here. Unless you count the coke blizzard."

She was supposed to laugh at that. A few years ago she would have.

"I don't think we can make it at all this weekend. The airports are closed. It's supposed to be worse than the blizzard of '78. Remember? I couldn't get a plane back to New York for five days."

"Of course I remember. I loved every minute of it."

"Me, too." She really had. What had happened to them?

"How's Antonia? What's with Skeeter? Can't wait to see you guys."

"Tone—the blizzard. Remember?"

"But Christy, tomorrow is my birthday," said his little boy voice.

"I know, love. Tell it to the snow god."

"Chris, promise to call me every couple of hours, keep me posted on the storm, okay? What's it doing there right now?"

"Snowing like crazy. I can barely see the street."

"What kind of snow?"

"White. You know."

"What *kind*. Fluffy? Granular? Wet? Is it sticking?"

"It sure is. Four inches since lunch."

"That's rubber cement."

Christy laughed. She'd always loved his sense of humor, corny as he was. The one big thing they'd always agreed on was that a sense of humor was the most important thing in life.

Tone wanted someone to take care of him. In that respect, he was just like the kids, maybe worse. Who was there to take care of her? But she knew the answer, damn it. They were both too headstrong. He wanted his way, she wanted hers. And neither of them wanted to give up anything. Not even to get what they both wanted most: Each other.

It was so exasperating. She'd been there for Tone, for the kids. Maybe not as often as they would have liked, or as she would have liked.

They loved her but they weren't understanding of her pressures and problems. Why?

That was one thing about a career: No one loved you. At *Allure*, they wanted your head, your job, your office. It was so much easier to deal with than blind love, with its guilt and confusion and ambivalence.

God, she was tired.

Her assistant had breezed out, never to return. Her boss was shacked up in Greenwich Village with the publisher. Apparently Skeeter was zonked out on the living room carpet and she couldn't go home and read him the riot act. Even if she could, it wouldn't affect him one way or the other, and besides, she had to see a hopeful creature who "wanted to get into beauty." A middle-aged male author who wrote under, God forbid, women's names, and wanted to broaden his horizons. At this rate Nanook of the North, probably in drag, would storm in any second.

"Christy? Are you there, Chris?"

"I'm here." She wished she weren't. She wished she were there.

Tone wanted someone to take care of him. Skeeter wanted someone to take care of him. Antonia wanted someone to take care of her. Who was going to take care of Christy? Suddenly she wanted to hang up.

"Take care, darling. I'll call just as soon as I know something definite about the planes."

"Let me play you the chorus to my song. Just once more. You're sure you really like it, Chris?"

"I really do. I think you've got a hit."

"...who says you cain't charge happ-i-ness?" When the tape was finished, Tone hung up.

His song was good. Just as good as anything she'd done at *Allure*. Maybe better. Why hadn't she been nicer to him? Why couldn't she get off the fence about quitting when deep down inside, she knew she couldn't live without her work?

It still wasn't too late for a New Year's resolution.

"I resolve to stop threatening to quit, to be nicer to Tone and...to be nicer to *me*."

Should she write it down? No. Jamie would find it and the verbal bulletin board would race into action.

Christy glanced at the small enamel clock on her desk, gift of Principessa Volponi, Ltd., fighters of cellulite. Where was Jamie? And Flemming Lord? She'd give him exactly five more minutes and then she was going home.

There was a package from Helena Rubenstein on her desk. It must have arrived while she was out on her non-lunch date with Juneau. Jamie never opened anything unless it looked interesting. Oh, well.

"*Burning Copper Volcano* powder eyeshadow," Christy read aloud as she opened the compact. Two sultry shades, double-ended applicator with sponge and brush.

Deftly, she whisked the darker shade into the crease between her brow and lid and filled in above with the lighter of the red shades. "Not bad. If you like conjunctivitis."

"Very becoming."

Christy wheeled around.

"Oh. You must be Mr. Flemming." Christy was flustered. She'd always hated surprises.

"Flemming Lord." He extended his hand and she grabbed it—a bit too quickly, too hard. What was wrong with her?

Flemming Lord could make you forget your social security number. He was the kind of breathtakingly stunning man who instantly made people say "Oh, he must be gay. They just don't make straight guys that gorgeous."

"If I'm going to work for you, don't you think we should be on a first name basis?"

Tough toenails, Tallulah. This guy's got some pair of balls. Juneau would love him. She'd offer him a drink.

"You look like you could use a drink, Mr. Lord."

He brushed some snow from his thick, curly, blond hair.

"Cognac, if you have it. I feel like I've just come through the St. Bernard Pass in my underwear."

Ah. A stab at being amusing. "Coming up. You might need this, too."

Christy threw him a towel. *Body Toner Terries* from Ms. Jogger. Christy had never heard of Ms. Jogger. It never ceased to amaze her—every hour, more new, expensive, unnecessary things arrived in her office. Who would buy them? Who would sell them?

Flemming Lord blotted his hair with the towel before taking a hefty bite out of the cognac.

Christy studied him. Rarely did she study a man. Makeup. Clothes. Hemlines. Hairstyles. But rarely men. There just weren't that many real ones around to study. Tone in his revealing bikini and Skeeter in his tennis grays didn't count.

Flemming Lord was a young Stewart Granger. She'd seen a rerun of *King Solomon's Mines* late last Wednesday. But no. His profile was more like the Twenties Arrow Shirt Man. He had thick lashes. Pure gold. Thick eyebrows to match.

He was wearing a tweed jacket, brown-and-purple checked shirt and polka dot bow tie.

Flemming Lord had to be in love with himself, along with every woman he'd ever so much as glanced at. It was making her very nervous.

He sat in her guest chair, an expectant look on his face. Was he tanned? Or was it bronzer? She wanted to touch his face. She must be losing her mind—never, ever had she wanted to touch a stranger's face.

Why had the weather conspired against her? Why had Tiff quit at exactly the wrong time? Why had Juneau decided to take this afternoon off and leave her here at the mercy of this...this...this person?

"Well, Mr....er...Flemming, tell me about yourself. I've read your letter, of course."

"I'm a writer. I write women's books. Romance. I don't suppose you've read *The Countess of Connaught*? Or *The Bastard of Belgrave Square*?"

Christy shook her head. She was beginning to wish she had. She smiled. Thank God for the four thousand dollars she'd spent on her front teeth—it had been worth every cent, every second of agony.

"Of course, what I write is pure shit. But then, as we all know, shit sells." Flemming Lord smiled back. *His* teeth weren't capped.

"All too true. Especially in the beauty business."

"You're not what I expected," he said bluntly. "Not at all."

Christy squirmed. What *had* he expected?

"I'm not?"

"No. No oversized lavender sunglasses. No absurd hat."

"No blue fox scarf," she added. "No Vuitton attaché with a diaphragm in it." Good God, what had made her say *that*?

62

"Yes. That's the general idea," he chuckled.

Christy had never actually heard anyone chuckle before. "I guess I'd expected someone quite different, too."

"Different from me? Or, well, you know, *different*?"

"As in 'poor dear, he's always been different.'" Christy giggled. Why was she giggling? She hated gigglers.

Back to business. "Why are you considering switching careers, Flemming?"

"I'm not actually thinking of switching. I intend to keep on writing, but I thought I might be able to gain some added insight into women if I were able to get a job in a woman's field."

It certainly made sense. "This business takes a lot out of you, Flemming. You might not have anything left over. Energy, I mean."

"I've always been pretty energetic, Christy," he said, fixing her with his great big brown eyes.

I just bet you have. Stop doing your wizardry on me. It won't work. Shit. It *was* working.

"I write a novel in two weeks. I used to hang my walls with brown paper and write standing up but I finally succumbed and bought a word processor."

"What dedication. I'd never be able to do that."

"You'd be surprised at what you could do, Christy." Again those insinuating eyes.

"What do you think you could do for me, Flemming?" Damn. Why had she asked it that way?

"I can write absolutely anything. So I suppose I could take a lot of pressure off there. I understand you travel. I'm fluent in French, Spanish, Italian, German and Greek. That might come in handy. I know a lot about the psychology of women but I think I can learn more. And I'll work under any name you like. I have no shame about *noms de plume*." He helped himself to another cognac.

Or about anything else, obviously. Who the hell did he think he was?

"Do you think you could stand it here? A lot of ladies. Lavender sunglasses. Lots of guys. More lavender sunglasses. Large helpings of jealousy, intramural fighting. Backbiting. Most of the time, everyone has his worst foot forward. And the pay is less than your prep school allowance."

Flemming Lord smiled. He must have spent hours in front of the bathroom mirror practicing.

"When can I start?"

"Monday. You could start tomorrow but I think with this snow, the office'll be closed."

Who was this person, using her voice to tell the dazzling Flemming Lord that he was hired?

She tried to think clearer. Just because he was hired didn't mean he couldn't be fired.

He leaned forward.

"Maybe we could have a drink together to celebrate? That is if you're not too busy?"

He would make an impact at *Allure*. Everybody would want to steal him. It had happened last year when one of the temp secretaries turned out to be a gorgeous college football player. From Juneau down, everyone of every conceivable sexual preference had fought to take him to lunch.

Oh, the hell with it. Her children were ransacking the house, her husband was splashing around in his pool with God only knew who, and she was sick and tired of being alone.

"Yes. Yes. That would be very nice."

"Where do you live? In this weather, I should get you as close to your home as possible."

"Seventy-second and Park."

"I live at Seventy-third and Lexington. Funny I haven't

64

ever seen you walking around the neighborhood."

That annoyed her.

"I'm terribly busy, Flemming. I don't have time to walk around the neighborhood."

"Oh, I meant on weekends. You know."

"I spend my weekends in Beverly Hills."

Flemming stared at her. "Beverly Hills? Does *Allure* have a branch out there?"

"No. But I do. My husband. Tone Shaw."

"The songwriter?"

"Yes—but I didn't think he was known for his songs. He's only been at it a year. He's a show biz lawyer. His songs are just a hobby."

"I like "Bev Hills Babe" a lot."

"That...song...about...the Rolls-Royce?" Christy thought it was the most boring song she'd ever heard. "Beverly Hills Babe, take me cruisin' to the beach." If there were other words, she'd never heard them. But maybe she was being unfair....

———————

An hour later, they arrived, sodden, frozen, teeth chattering, at Flemming Lord's apartment. Before they left Christy's office, he had slipped the half-empty bottle of cognac into the pocket of his enormous British overcoat. It had kept them alive, Christy was convinced of it.

"First, we make a fire," Flemming announced. "I think you should hop right into a hot tub, Christy."

Hot tub. Tone was probably in his right now. Damn. Did she really want to do this?

Flemming's living room was dominated by an enormous Tudor four-poster hung with flame stitch needlepoint, heavily moth-eaten. There were two director's chairs, sagging. A Queen Anne loveseat. A wobbly card table. An oak refectory table containing parts of the word processor. And a wheezing electric typewriter he had forgotten to turn off.

"Not exactly the Bastard of Belgrave Square's drawing room, is it?"

"Much more character, Flemming." Christ, would she ever get used to that ridiculous name? But this *was* an adventure. It was fun. A hell of a lot more fun than listening to Juneau's put-downs, Skeeter's whining, Antonia's prim reprimands and Tone's passionate declarations of eternal randiness from 3,000 miles away. That reminded her—she should call him. But what for? Another weather report? They had television sets in Beverly Hills, God knew.

She flopped into one of Flemming's director's chairs.

"Now, you're beginning to see why my affair with romance novels is beginning to cool down. You're probably the only person, other than my typist, pardon, my word processor operator, who's been in here in eons."

What was he telling her? No glamorous female companion slipped in of an evening to fix him dinner, massage away the eyestrain? She was here, wasn't she? She'd thought of mentioning *Jack's,* the black-and-white two-story restaurant across the street. But she hadn't. She'd followed Flemming Lord like a Chinese wife. She inched closer to the enormous limestone fireplace and pulled off her squishy boots.

"Now, about that drink? Champagne? Scotch? Or vodka? I'm afraid we've killed off your cognac."

"Champagne." Somehow it seemed safer than Scotch or vodka. Now that she was beginning to warm up, she felt dizzy from the brandy. "And a glass of water."

"Perrier?"

"Sure."

Flemming sat in the chair across from her.

"There's something about me you don't know, Christy."

"You're afraid you don't have any talent."

Christy had always been like that—she could sense things about people, and sometimes she just blurted it out. For a moment Flemming looked surprised.

"I was a fat kid from Cape May, New Jersey. I wore glasses. Thick, bulgy ones with pale frames. I was so fat that the fat hung out of my khaki shorts in...in lumps."

Why was he telling her this?

He pulled a mangy snapshot from his wallet. Christy stared at it. On the back was written, in fading green ink: "Bibby, Camp Nessapeak, 1961." Bibby was about five feet tall and weighed about one hundred eighty.

"I used to keep it on the refrigerator door. Now I keep it in my wallet. For when I'm in restaurants."

"Restaurants?"

"I always look at it before I send back the rolls and butter."

"Oh." Maybe she could write a diet article about that. On second thought, maybe *he* could write it. Christy weighed one hundred ten and had never dieted in her life.

"I think you should write about it for the magazine, Flemming. Readers love sharing diet experiences. Next to what to do about fine, thin hair."

"OK," he sipped his champagne, "I will. Cheers, Christy. I think we're going to get along famously."

Unfortunately, he was probably right.

"Here's to *you*, Flemming." She raised her glass. Did he look so good because everything else in her life lately had been so bad?

She'd long since rejected the idea of casual sex. What was worse than waking up in a strange bed, with a stranger person? She'd tried it a few times over the past few years. Out of need. Curiosity. Boredom. Retaliation when she'd imagined Tone's latest exploits. The medicine had been worse than the disease.

She leaned back. At last she was beginning to relax. She gazed at Flemming Lord, his blond hair burnished by the firelight. Why should Jamie Doran have him?

Maybe he was really just interested in his new job.

That was a sobering thought. Was this the role-reversal version of the casting couch?

She was in charge. *She* was the boss. *She* was calling the shots. All Flemming had done was to manipulate her into position so that she could call a few more.

Reed Doran had confided to her that this had happened to him. Bright Young Things, afraid that their education, backgrounds and fresh faces weren't enough to make it at *Allure*, had propositioned him many times. He claimed that he'd always turned them down.

Christy studied Flemming. He barely seemed to be breathing, much less making a move toward her. Why wasn't he? At least he could try.

The old insecurities flooded back. Must be the champagne. She hadn't had any lunch. She'd had a cognac. Now, she wished she'd eaten something.

Damn Juneau for canceling.

"Do you like England, Flemming?"

"The most civilized country on earth for two thousand years?"

"I love it. Everyone doesn't. The rain. Arabs."

"That's like saying you don't like New York City because of the dirt and the muggers." He crossed one impossibly long leg over the other.

They both knew the moment had fled. The champagne was gone. The fire was dying. There was a long silence. "I think I better go home," Christy said slowly.

"Why don't you call?"

Christy laughed. "I can tell you don't have any children, Flemming."

"Oh? How?"

"Checking on teenagers over the phone is like—well, calling a burglar while he's robbing your apartment."

Flemming laughed and stood up. He held out his hands. "OK. I'll walk you home."

"No, really, it's only around the corner."

She was glad it was too dark for Flemming to see her blush. She wanted to escape—he was too dangerous for her in her present state of mind.

———————

It was even colder out now and the two-block walk to 72nd and Park took an eternity.

She wasn't looking forward to confronting the kids. When something went wrong, they always ganged up on her. The Kurtz kid would probably be there, too. He practically lived with them, making it even harder for her to blow her stack. Oh, well, there was something to be said for self-control.

Six

Beverly Hills

At first, Tone thought that Christy might have been exaggerating the snowstorm in New York. But no, God-damn it to hell, there *was* a blizzard. Nothing was landing and no one knew when anything would. He'd spent the better part of an hour on the phone to Eastern. The 9:35 wasn't taking off tonight. Neither were the ten o'clock flights from American, TWA and United.

As he hung up for the last time, it hit him—what about Washington, D.C.?

After twenty frustrating minutes of listening to various recordings telling him to please stand by, Tone called Eastern Airlines in Washington. Planes were landing. Tone didn't wait to hear the schedules. He tore into his bedroom, grabbed his Vuitton hang-up bag, stuffed dinner clothes, a tweed jacket, three ties and his toilet kit into it before he realized that he wasn't taking a trip; he was going to his other home.

Why was Christy always bitching about packing? He didn't even have to take a toothbrush.

God, this was exciting. He hadn't been to New York in almost two years. New York in the snow.... It brought back memories of his childhood in North Andover, Massachusetts.

What others had called bitter cold, his mother had referred to as brisk. Well, brisk had driven him three thousand miles away. He really should call her. Sarah-Jane Grantland Shaw. His birthday had proved to the world she had made love at least once in her chilly uneventful life.

Not knowing when he'd return, he called a cab. The Rolls would rest much easier in the garage with the burglar alarm on. He whistled as he poured a Scotch to help him through the trauma of putting on his socks. He hadn't worn socks since...since when?

As he strolled down the blue stone path that connected his front patio to Rodeo Drive, Tone had an eerie feeling that he was on the verge on something new, big and unknown.

But maybe he was just being dumb. Most people go through their lives feeling as though they're on the brink of something wonderful, new, exciting and it never happens. Just the same old rut.

SEVEN

New York City

CHRISTY KNEW she could fall in love with Flemming Lord. She also knew that she didn't have the time. It would take her away from her career, her children— she'd come to think of Skeeter as hers—and what little time she had for Tone. But the prospect *was* appealing. Anyway, she was curious. That was it. *Curious.* What was under that tweed jacket and bow tie and plaid shirt?

But with all his good looks, Flemming wasn't overtly sexy. It was more of an animal magnetism. He had a maddeningly attractive way of fixing his eyes on you and peering into your soul.

Somehow he had willed her to hire him. She knew it was a mistake even as she'd said the words. How in hell was she going to work with Flemming Lord day in, day out?

Oh, he'd take orders. That wasn't what she was worried about. He'd probably do a great job, too. And if she did decide to go to bed with him, he didn't seem like the type who would ever discuss it with anyone. Not that there were any secrets at *Allure*. Everyone had known about Juneau and Reed for years and it hadn't made a damn bit of difference. No one even talked about it anymore.

Christ, what was she thinking of? She had to pack. Round up the kids. Try to get on a flight to Los Angeles.

Tone had no patience with snowstorms or missed planes. Or anything, for that matter, that delayed instant gratification. And on his fiftieth birthday, he was sure to be more demanding than usual.

The birthday party. All those creeps he loved. The loser-students of drama, speech and voice-overs. That asshole Jake Witt he kept talking about. The greatest thing to happen to music since The Stones. It always depressed her when things that should be fun took on the pall of business obligations.

Christy squinted into the night. She might have been at the North Pole, the South Pole, silent upon a peak in Darien. Just one more block and she could dump her soggy clothes and slip into a hot bath. Without Mr. Flemming Lord....

The snow had cleared her head and she half-dreaded going upstairs. She always suspected the worst when any one of them was evasive on the telephone. Now she was beginning to feel guilty about having drinks with Flemming Lord. Why? She hadn't done anything wrong. But she'd *considered* it. Anyhow, every time she was somewhere enjoying herself, something horrible happened at home.

When she'd been in Grasse, Skeeter had set his bed on fire. When she'd gone to Milan, Antonia had fallen skating in the Park and needed eighteen stitches across her kneecap. One of the weekends she couldn't make it to L.A., Tone had slipped in the pool and broken his leg. Naturally, it was all her fault.

She nodded to the doorman and dripped across the lobby to the elevator. Had he given her a funny look or was it her imagination?

Cautiously, she inserted her key in the lock, opened

74

the door and stepped into the apartment. The living room didn't look too bad. Ed was scrubbing the rug with something that looked like raspberry Kool Aid.

How in hell had they managed to break her favorite Regency chair?

"OK, kids. What's been going on here?"

Antonia regarded her mother with her usual insolent cool.

"Tell me exactly what happened, Antonia." Christy stripped off her coat and rubbed her wet curls with a towel she kept in the closet.

"The boys were in the living room, goofing off. I was packing. I heard a noise. One of the boys fell into your antique chair. That's about it."

Antonia did have a strange maturity. At least she always told the unvarnished truth.

Ed struggled toward the kitchen door, the bucket and a roll of paper towel clutched to his chest. "At least the rug no longer looks as though it were imported from the heart of Kazak, Mrs. Shaw."

What's *that* supposed to mean, Christy wondered.

Antonia tugged at her sleeve.

"Guess what, Mother?"

"I couldn't guess who's buried in Grant's tomb."

"Ed is going to California with us."

"That is if it's OK," Ed added, dumping the bucket into the sink.

Why not? He practically lived with them anyway.

"It's OK with me. But is it OK with your mother?"

Apparently the kids had worked it all out. And right now, she didn't need them as enemies. When Ed was around, Antonia and Skeeter were much nicer to her.

"My mother is so happy to get rid of me that she'd give us a limo to L.A.—that is, if we could get through the snow drifts."

Ed's mother probably did want to get rid of him. He was always upstairs with Skeeter and Antonia when he was home from school. What was so fascinating about her apartment? Mrs. Kurtz must be a lot less strict about house rules.

Strict. Look at the living room. What had they really been doing all afternoon? Skeeter was usually very neat. His room looked like no one ever slept in it. Antonia was Ms. Perfection. Even her drawers were neat.

"Come on, Ed, I'm sure your mother doesn't want to get rid of you. How *is* she, anyway? I haven't seen her this week."

"The same, I guess. Waiting on the nerd, hand and foot."

"Oh, Ed." Antonia sighed. "You shouldn't call him...Mr. Clarkson, I mean...names."

"I'm not sure that nerd qualifies as a name, exactly. I think it's an adjective and an apt one at that."

"It's not polite, Ed."

"How about Van Nerdwell, then? More class."

"Ed-mund, let's change the subject."

"OK, Antonia. How would you like it if you came home day after day to find your old lady, excuse me, your mother shacked up with a bossy, supercilious, skinny creep, ten years older than you, whose only claim to fame is that he was president of his high school senior class, somewhere in the hinterlands of New Jersey?"

"Maybe you have a point, Ed. *Maybe.*"

"Of course I have a point. Your dad just *happens* to head up his own organization. Nerdwell can just about make it through his chores. You know—the groceries, cleaner, pick up two copies of the *Times* so they can have crossword puzzle races with their coffee and croissants. Class president. Ha. I'm just glad about one thing, Antonia."

76

"What?"

"That I'm not related to the shit."

"Cheer up, Ed," grinned Skeeter, crashing through the door, stomping snow and ice all over the foyer. "Maybe your mom is expecting the patter of little feet."

"The only little feet in 8-C belong to the roaches. Nerdwell doesn't have what it takes. Remember the oft-quoted Cantonese proverb: 'Watch out for the man whose stomach doesn't move when he laughs.' That's our man."

Christy couldn't believe what she was hearing. Did they always talk like this to each other? How had she managed to raise a daughter with the sensibilities of a 19th-century virgin? Skeeter and Ed were sixteen; Antonia, eight. They hadn't yet been cursed with the coyness, the angora personality of a Jamie Doran or a Tiffany Thomas. Maybe they never would.

Antonia was tugging at her again.

"Mother? Aren't we going to the Coast?"

"I don't see how we can, darling." As of four o'clock, absolutely nothing was taking off. It was now almost seven and the weather, if anything, looked worse.

"I know how we can, Christy," said Skeeter, slipping another film cartridge into his camera. "We take the Metroliner to Washington and take off for L.A. from there. So simplistic even a magazine publisher could overlook it."

It was the most intelligent thing Christy had heard all day. "You may have something there, Skeeter. Is anybody packed?"

"I am, Mother." Antonia, of course. She was permanently packed. "I put a few things out for you, too. And all Daddy's presents are packed. Ed is getting packed. As for Skeeter, who knows."

Christy studied the Amtrak schedule to Washington. Every hour from two 'til six. Forget that.

"With this weather, Mother, nothing will be on time. Let's just go down to Penn Station and hang out. It'll be fun."

Hanging out in Penn Station fun? But maybe she was right. At least they'd be moving. Not just sitting there waiting for something to happen.

Christy went to the phone and dialed Tone. After eleven rings she hung up. She called the limousine service Juneau and Reed used. They didn't promise anything. They'd try. *Try.* God, there was that word again.

Skeeter and Antonia were whispering. "Are you ready, Skeeter?"

"Almost."

Christy checked his room. His chaos was as meticulously organized as the Dewey Decimal System. Chests and boxes, each labeled in black Magic Marker, were piled to the ceiling along three walls. On the window wall, the boxes rose to the window sills. Here, Skeeter kept whatever was his mania of the moment. This week's mania was a snake, Doctor Watson. Nine feet long with dark brown diamonds on a tan background. It eyed Christy malevolently from its glass case.

"Doctor Watson has to go to L.A., Christy," Skeeter said with conviction. "He has to. Something might happen to him."

"What could happen to him?"

"Well, he might get out. Get lost."

"How could he get out?"

"If the doorman put some packages in our apartment and he wasn't watching, Doctor Watson might wiggle out into the hall and get lost."

"That's ridiculous."

"Well, suppose Marlene came in to clean up. She could accidentally let him out the back door. It wouldn't be the first time. Please...."

78

What was one more boa constrictor on the Metroliner?

"OK. Let's get packing." Christy sighed. This trip was going to be fun if it killed her.

Eight

Washington, D.C.

THERE WAS a blizzard in New York.

The British Airways Concorde from London had to land at Dulles International Airport instead of Kennedy. As a general groan went up, a clipped voice apologized profusely and promised to help with transportation and hotel accommodations.

Bette Farmington couldn't have cared less. She slipped her jeweled hand through the crook of Ian Harrington's charcoal flannel arm and squeezed.

The insolent, amusing, sexy Ian was the nicest prize Bette had ever won in all her years of playing killer, high-stakes international backgammon.

Two days before, Bette had originally booked on the Concorde to New York and TWA to L.A. for her ex-husband Tone Shaw's fiftieth birthday party.

Harrington had met his match in Bette. With her strident voice, overkill jewelry, hair streaked blonde in twelve shades, she was only tolerated because she was such a good gambler and those who lost were more than anxious to win back their money.

It was rumored that Bette had won her jewels—among them Marie of Romania's emerald tiara—her clothes

81

and flat. No one knew if she'd won the Rolls. Some speculated that it had been given to her for keeping her three-shades-of-pink mouth shut.

Bette and Ian had played through the night, until lunch Wednesday, when Ian realized that he'd lost an entire year's stipend from his trust fund plus his airline ticket back to New York.

"Well, Ian," Bette said, turning the doubling die to 512, "how about it? Or are the stakes a bit high for you?"

Bette was the queen of all cunts. She made his ex-wife Jill look like Peter Pan. Winning this game was his only prayer of winning back anything. He had to take the double. It wasn't that bad. How could he have known that Bette would throw double-sixes four times in a row? What were the odds of that happening? It made him sick just thinking about it.

"I think we should knock off for lunch, Ian," Bette suggested, her voice dulled to a croak from last night's Scotch and cigarettes. "Why don't we shower and see if we can book at Wilton's—you know. Bury Street, right off Jermyn, down past Turnbull & Asser?"

Ian knew it well. It was one of his favorites. Fresh salmon flown in from Scotland in the middle of the night. Velvet draperies and lace curtains. The tiniest of bars. One half expected Thackeray to step in and order a plate of oysters. Finally he'd found someone to pick up the hefty tab.

"I'll call them, Bette. 930-8391, if I recall. And since you've won all my money, it's your treat."

"You're so...quaint, Ian," Bette smiled. She had him just where she wanted him: at her mercy. She hadn't had a live-in, unpaid companion in some time and it did make things so much easier. Bette hated eating in restaurants by herself. She hated answering the telephone. Her maid, wonderful at everything, wouldn't take messages. Ian would. She liked his voice. Resonant. Cultured. Theirs could blossom into a symbiotic relationship. Love? It had been so long since Bette Farmington had been in love that she'd almost forgotten it existed. Damn. She had a dreadful headache. The shower would get rid of it. Ian. Men.

They were the opponents. Bette's whole being was geared to winning. When she did lose it was only to give her opponents a false sense of security. Ian had fallen for it. First he'd felt overly confident. He'd had too much to drink. She'd let him win more than $5,000. He'd been gleeful. About this time she'd decided his true age was somewhere between ten and sixteen, her son's age. In fact, Skeeter was far more mature than Ian Harrington. At least Skeeter could see through her.

Bette stripped off her clothes and stepped into Pumpkin's shower. Six shower heads pelted hot and cold water onto her aching body. She was a fool to keep on playing. At forty-five, her stamina was beginning to decline. Last week she'd read somewhere that people were beginning to live to be one hundred. One thing was for sure—she couldn't take fifty-five more years of backgammon.

As she soaped her stomach, Ian Harrington stepped into the shower beside her and took over. Without asking. How dare he?

"I presume this isn't your first shower liaison?"

"Do you want me to leave? I refuse. I had no idea what was under your Valentino."

"How did you know it was a Valentino?"

"I looked at the label."

"You certainly get it all out up front, love."

"I'll let that one go by, Bette. In the meantime, I'm working up a tremendous appetite."

So was she. She hadn't bothered much about sex these past few years. Too much backgammon and house-guesting.

She was sought after because she played so well.

Everything else about her made hostesses wince. But at least they didn't have to worry about Bette trying to steal their husbands or lovers. All she seemed to be interested in was the game.

Ian lifted her against him and pressed his mouth to hers. She felt wonderful. Warm. Wet. Slippery. His erection reached toward her. She slid her long silken fingers beneath it and guided it toward her. The hell with her hair.

As Ian thrust into her, Bette's foot slipped on the soapy tile and they both fell backwards under the showerhead's steamy torrent.

He tried to help her up. It was impossible. They were like a pair of walruses slithering in the mud at the watering hole. Ian laughed. It wasn't the sort of thing one mentioned to one's almost conquest.

Bette didn't think it was so funny.

"This is about the most unromantic interlude I've ever been involved in." When she finally got out and began to towel herself dry, she felt two of her ribs. She'd had cracked ribs once before and now she was certain that it had happened again. So much for passion.

———————

After a lunch of cold Scottish salmon, chocolate torte and a bottle of champagne, Bette was able to broach the subject of Ian's financial situation.

"What are you going to do, Ian? I can't leave you in London without a pound to your name."

"Plenty of people would, Bette," he said, thinking of Jill, of his daughter, Beth, of his late grandmother. All the people who tried "to talk sense into him." What was the difference between Bette and his ex-wife, Jill? Or his other ex-wife, what-was-her-name? Juliet. Or Helen, the most boring woman he'd ever fucked.

All women could be manipulated. Even Bette Farmington. He'd let her beat him at backgammon just so she could think she had the upper hand. Now she'd pay.

He studied Bette's face. She might have been chiseled from flint or granite. Her thin lips barely parted when she spoke. Her eyes regarded you as though you were something on exhibit. Something that might lay an egg or devour its mate or copulate for five hours. Dispassionate but not quite disinterested. He longed to melt the facade. But what if that's all there was?

A thousand questions ran through Ian's mind. Where was Bette's ex-husband, the famous Tone Shaw? Must have been an asshole to have married her. A horror, no doubt. And her son, Skeeter? Was there any real money behind the backgammon bravado?

"I think I cracked my ribs when I fell in the shower, Ian. It feels like hell." She shifted her weight in the plush Victorian chair.

Ian said he was sorry and ordered another bottle of champagne.

"I might as well ask you, Ian."

"Ask me what?" Here it comes, he thought. She's finally going to offer to buy me a ticket back to New York.

"Why don't you come back to New York with me? Bet we can get on the Concorde tomorrow morning. It's never fully booked."

He pretended surprise.

"Why not?"

What else did he have to do? Shower. Change his clothes. Go out to lunch. Go out to dinner. Wangle invitations to the opera, the theater. Anything. Play bridge. Play backgammon.

"But, Bette, I would like a chance to recoup some of my money."

"We have the rest of tonight and three hours in the

morning on our way to New York. That should be time enough."

"I guess so." He wasn't convinced.

"Let's make a deal, Ian. If I win the next six games, after we get back to Pumpkin's, I win you for...say...six months."

"Let's make it an even dozen games. I want to give myself every advantage. And let's make it for a year. You and I have a lot in common, Bette. We could have a hell of a good time."

"I think you may be right, Ian." Smiling, Bette raised her glass to her perfectly penciled lips.

NINE

Somewhere near Washington

THE METROLINER smelled of rancid orange juice and stale cigarette smoke.

Skeeter, his face stuck into a copy of *Omni*, was lost in black holes while Dr. Watson, phylum Chordata, subphylum Vertebrata, class Reptilia, order Squamata, family Boidae, dozed fitfully in his camera case on the floor.

Antonia and Ed Kurtz were playing Spite & Malice.

Christy was gnawing on a cheese sandwich that must have been exhumed from the Great Pyramid, washing it down with a vodka martini. Ordinarily, she didn't drink martinis. Too dangerous. But tonight—well, tonight was different.

Four tickets. First class. Ha. For one hundred ninety-six dollars people were sitting on suitcases, standing, leaning against the walls. They had one thing in common besides their destination: eating. Hostess Twinkies du jour. Gourmet peanut butter and jelly crackers. Danish with icing as hard as the rime on the outside of the window.

She ordered another martini and then felt guilty about it. Screw it. She needed a break.

She opened her attaché and began to go through it.

They were somewhere near Philadelphia, so she had about two hours to clean it out completely. She reread the details of the trip to Bath scheduled for June. Her mind was made up. She'd take the kids and let the chips fall where they may. This time, she'd stick to her resolve. After the trip, she'd deal with whether or not she'd stay on at *Allure*. No more discussions with Juneau.

She'd spent so much time these past weeks resifting her life. She used to like her job; she used to be in love with Tone; she *used* to be able to control Skeeter and Antonia. Where did it end? Did other women go through this? She'd thought of confiding in friends at *Allure* but had always stopped herself.

Juneau would have given her two tickets to the ballet and told her to cheer up. And none of Christy's assistants had any children, much less husbands. Their problems revolved around getting someone into bed, multiple orgasms, clothes in "W" and experimenting with the new products that arrived daily at *Allure*. Other than Marcy Kurtz, Ed's mother, Christy had no one to talk to about anything.

She'd had a drink with Marcy last week. Marcy, whose attention span was about as long as it took to spray cheese on a Ritz Cracker, had opened the conversation with "When you're my age (forty-eight), you'll be whistling a different tune." Christy, whose favorite tune was "I Love New York," had agreed.

Apparently Mr. Kurtz had had the nerve to die, leaving Marcy a woman alone, at the mercy of fortune hunters, like her live-in lover. "Ed hates him, you know. I don't know what I can do about it. I'm almost afraid to go to sleep in my own apartment. Know what I mean?"

"Don't be silly, Marcy. We've got wonderful security here. And you've got Ed to protect you."

"Ed sleeps at your apartment."

Christy knew that Ed slept over a lot. But every night?

"I hadn't realized, Marcy. I'll send him home."

"Please don't. Not if he doesn't bother you. Frank can't stand him." She'd looked like she was about to burst into tears but Marcy usually looked like she was about to burst into tears. "What do you do when the two most important men in your life despise each other?"

Christy tried to think of an answer. Tone and Skeeter loved each other. "I don't know, Marcy. I guess...I guess that isn't one of my problems." She'd wanted to add "Thank God," but thought better of it.

She yawned. The martinis were taking effect. Or maybe it was thinking about Marcy Kurtz. She was so typical of all the middle-aged woman who wrote in to *Allure* for beauty advice—all insecure, afraid to try anything new, convinced their lives were over at forty or forty-five or fifty.

Christy wanted to help them and spent many hours on her replies to their letters. Juneau's answers were laced with bland pop psychology, and rehashed beauty "secrets" that she herself supposedly employed. Juneau insisted that everyone from *Allure* who answered a letter enclose a photograph of herself to inspire confidence in the reader, so Christy had commissioned Francesco Scavullo to do the portraits. She was convinced it had only made the readers more miserable.

Shit. She'd forgotten about Tone's birthday present. She'd planned on doing some shopping on Rodeo Drive—his favorite store was *Bijan Pakzad*, probably the most expensive men's store in the world. For snobbery, it was certainly second to none. She hoped Jamie had called to make her appointment. Bijan hated tourists pawing the merchandise, and Christy had never seen more than one other person in the shop, looking for the perfect thing. Bijan custom-made every one of his creations; no knock-offs by the thousands.

But Tone already owned so many of his things. $400 cotton shirts, $1,800 alligator shoes, a $300 scarf. What was left? The $98,000 king-size bedspread made from matched chinchilla skins? If he expected that, he'd have to top the charts with a couple of hit songs.

Christy closed her eyes. She'd been so tired lately. She really ought to see the doctor. Tone ran to Dr. what's-his-name at the drop of a Kleenex.

The woman next to her sneezed and began rummaging in her bag. "Oh, dear. I don't suppose you have a Kleenex, do you? I think I'm coming down with something. All this snow. It's positively lethal."

Christy agreed about the snow. Thank God she was settled in beside an attractive woman in her thirties who seemed to have a lot of reading to do and not one of those old ladies who read a newspaper for five minutes before launching into an interminable monologue. Maybe Ms. Sniffles would blow her nose and nod discreetly over her work. At least the kids were quiet and Skeeter hadn't called anyone dumb for several hours.

"Do you go to Washington often?" the woman asked Christy.

"No, I don't." Christy shuffled her papers, pretending to look for a pen.

"I go twice a month. More if I have to. But the trip is so enervating. Know what I mean?"

Christy nodded sagely.

"You see, my husband, Arthur, lives in Washington."

"Oh?" Christy turned to her with fresh interest.

"Twice a month, I go to Washington and twice a month, he comes to New York to see me. We're lawyers."

"Why do you do that...commute?"

"Because my field, family relations, is more important here and Art's, government taxation, is more important there."

"Couldn't you get a job in Washington?"

"Sure. For half the money and twice the work. Unless you're a glorified clerk, you're better off in New York." The woman blew her nose again.

Christy fished out a clump of Kleenex and handed it to her. "How long have you been living apart?"

"Oh, we don't live apart. I mean, we're not separated or anything. We just happen to have two separate homes. People who've never tried it think we're nuts."

They were nuts.

"I'm Christy Shaw."

"And I'm Carrie. Carrie Hill. You know, your name sounds familiar. Have we met?"

"I don't think so. Do you read *Allure*?"

"It's my bible."

"That's where you've seen my name. I'm a beauty editor."

Carrie Hill looked impressed. "What a glamorous life. All those beautiful trips to far away places. The new makeup. The clothes. I seem to have slipped into the world of blue or black suits and white blouses. I think I'm wearing the same shade of lipstick I wore when I was sixteen."

Christy laughed. "It's not as glamorous as you might think. It's like the movies: *you* never see the set or the backdrops. *You* never hear anyone blowing his lines or blowing up. *You* never see anyone burning out. All you see is perfection. Some of our beautiful spreads on far away places cost what would be a year's income to an emerging Third World Nation. But, like they always say, what the reader doesn't see won't hurt her."

"Well, nothing is cheap these days. Especially Metro-liner tickets. Forty-five dollars per, one way. Sometimes I think I should ride my bicycle to D.C. Might be good for my figure."

She should try footing the bill for a few plane tickets.

"What new things are going to be coming out in *Allure*?" Carrie asked, peeping into Christy's attaché.

"Well, there's a new line of things for the bath called *The Wife of Bath* scheduled for spring—June."

"Does that mean you'll be going to Bath, in *England*?"

"Yes."

"Arthur and I haven't had a vacation in seven years. We spend all of our vacation money on Amtrak." She laughed.

"And you probably have children in...prep school?" Christy asked cautiously. How old was this Carrie Hill?

"Oh, no. Art and I don't have any children. We've discussed it. We just don't have time for them." Did Christy detect a little sadness in her voice?

She and Tone had never actually talked about having children. One morning she woke up so sick at her stomach that she thought she had food poisoning. Seven and a half months later, Antonia appeared. Maybe they *should* have discussed it. But she'd always wanted a child— especially a daughter. Suddenly she felt sorry for Carrie Hill.

"That's too bad."

Carrie smiled. "Oh it's all right. Neither of us could deal with children—even one child. We're in our offices eleven or twelve hours a day. When I get to Washington, I spend Saturday in bed, trying to catch up on sleep. When Art comes to New York, he does the same thing. Sundays, we read the papers together, go to a movie and then one of us is back on Amtrak. That's the way it's been for over ten years. We've been married for eleven." She blew her nose.

"What do you get out of it all?"

"I used to think it was prestige. Only woman partner in a law firm. You know. Then, after I got tired of prestige, it became fulfillment as in 'it's so much more fulfilling to spend six hours every weekend on a train than to spend six hours every weekend fixing a sensational dinner or entertaining your friends or going to the theater or opera.' I adore the opera. I've only been to three operas in eleven years and not with Art."

"Doesn't he like the opera?"

"Oh, yes, but he hasn't seemed to have time even for records since he was graduated from law school."

There were so many questions Christy was dying to ask Carrie Hill, especially about sex, but she couldn't bring herself to do it. She wished she had a dollar for every impertinent question perfect strangers had asked *her* on her European trips. Safe, sane well-mannered people seemed to lose all of their sanity and charm away from home.

"I'm boring you, Christy."

"Not at all." This was the most interesting conversation she'd had in weeks. Except maybe for the one with the incomparable Flemming Lord.

"Compared with what you do, what I do is extremely dull. I feel like I've been getting more and more boring by the week. It used to be by the year, then the month. Arthur hardly has anything to say to me any more."

That certainly wasn't Tone. He never stopped having things to talk about.

What does Arthur do besides read and work and not listen to the opera, Christy wanted to ask.

"You know, Christy, we don't even bother to make love any more. That's gotten too boring, too. Maybe you could write an article for *Allure* about sexless marriages? I can't believe I'm the only woman in the United States who's in one."

Christy scrutinized Carrie Hill. Early thirties. Good, firm figure. Shiny dark red hair. Nicely, if ultra-conservatively dressed. If only she'd sit up straight. The stoop of her shoulders conveyed sadness, depression...defeat? That was it. Defeat.

"How old are you, Carrie? I mean—our readers have a median age."

"I'm thirty."

"So am I. That means you were really young when you decided on your lifestyle. You know what I would have suggested if you'd written to me at *Allure* about your...problem?"

"Take a vacation."

"Right."

"I keep bringing it up. I've managed to save up five thousand dollars that Arthur doesn't know about just for a vacation. I mentioned it last weekend. He said it was a good idea and why didn't I get away for a few weeks."

"By yourself?"

"You got it. I'm by myself four nights a week as it is. My evenings are like an alcoholic desperately trying to get through cocktail hour without a drink. Sometimes, I call Arthur. Sometimes, he calls me. It only makes it worse. Ever wake up in the morning with the phone in the other side of the bed?" Carrie Hill turned watery green eyes to Christy.

It was the loneliest sentence Christy had ever heard.

"You should go to the opera more, Carrie."

"I did for a while. I met someone, you see...I really shouldn't have."

"Gone to the opera? Why not?"

"No, *met* someone. A guy. What's worse, a guy from the office. Another lawyer. He loves the opera, too."

It sounded innocent enough. Two lonely opera-lovers spending a night at Lincoln Center. Christy pictured herself sitting next to Flemming Lord, *La Traviata* washing over them.

"Things got out of hand. We fell in love. It was the worst thing that ever happened to me."

"What happened?"

"We made love. Went to the theater, the movies. Did all the things Arthur and I never seem to have time to do."

"Sounds great to me."

"It was great. We made love every night. Sometimes, at lunch. I felt wicked. Wonderful. And then, I began to hate myself."

"Guilt?" Christy was leaning toward Carrie, every muscle, every nerve, straining to hear her above the rattle of the wheels and the crackling of the Twinkies wrappers.

"More than that. I felt like I shouldn't be having fun when Arthur had his nose to the grindstone."

"So what did you do?"

"We stopped seeing each other. It was awful. We went to a restaurant. *Il Nido.* Know it? Gorgeous. Italian."

Did she know it. What a question.

"I said 'Craig, we can't go on like this,' and you know what he said?"

Christy shook her head.

"He said 'I agree with you. Get a divorce and marry me.' That simple. I couldn't handle it."

"Was he married?"

"No."

"Why didn't you do it? It sounds like you were having a much better life with him than with...Arthur."

"I was. I was. But I didn't deserve it. Don't you see?"

Christy didn't see. It made no sense to her at all. If that happened to her, she'd be very, very tempted to divorce Tone, even though he was nothing like the strange Arthur.

"Why do you want to punish yourself, Carrie?"

"Arthur paid for my law school. He encouraged me in my career. Don't you see? I owe him everything."

"You don't owe him your life. No one has the right to expect that."

"I guess not. Listen, I feel funny burdening you with all this." Carrie stood up. "Would you excuse me for a minute? Think I'll find a bathroom."

Christy rubbed her forehead. Her headache of this morning was returning with a vengeance. Had it only been this morning?

———

No one noticed that Doctor Watson had managed to crawl out of the camera case and was making his way under the seats, toward the front of the car. Of course, no one was expecting to see a boa constrictor on the Metroliner. He inched up into a seat and curled himself next to a white toy poodle. A long, piercing scream echoed through the car.

"What do you want?" the poodle's mistress demanded shrilly of Doctor Watson. "Get out of here."

The woman, in a pink Chanel suit and black fox hat, began hitting at Doctor Watson with a rolled-up newspaper. The snake backed down, staring at her.

Skeeter looked up from *Omni*. "Je-sus," he muttered. This was a job for Peter Lorre or Sidney Greenstreet or even George Sanders. They'd know how to brush off that idiotic woman like a fly in the tropics. He jumped to his feet and loped up the aisle, smiling, radiating charm. Now was no time for some ignorant conductor to give Doctor Watson the cement shoes. That is, if he'd worn shoes in the first place.

"Madame, allow me," he said, scooping Doctor Watson into his arms. "He must have gotten cabin fever in here. You know...claustro."

The woman's black fox hat was hanging over her left ear. "That vicious snake tried to attack Lord Snowden." She patted the poodle's soft white curls. "Lord Snowden is scared of snakes."

"No reason to be scared of Doctor Watson." Skeeter slid into the seat beside the woman. "Doctor Watson isn't poisonous. He wouldn't dare bite anyone. He isn't even hungry."

She looked half convinced.

"How do you know he's not hungry?"

"He ate yesterday."

"If I hadn't eaten since yesterday, young man, I'd be damn hungry." The poodle twitched against her ample bosom.

"Yes, ma'am," Skeeter answered, affecting his best Blair-Academy-before-he'd-been-kicked-out manners. "But boa constrictors eat only once a month."

"Ohhh."

Skeeter smiled and wound the snake around his arm. "I'll take him back to his case now. He's probably upset by all these people." He moved to stand up.

"What does he eat?" The poodle had stopped shaking and was beginning to yap at the top of its reedy little voice.

"I fed him a rat. Yesterday afternoon."

"That's disgusting. Positively disgusting."

"Are you a devotee of rats, ma'am?" Skeeter asked genially, and returned to his seat.

Christy had watched the whole performance in silence, ready to step in and take Skeeter's side against the harridan. But it hadn't been necessary. Was it possible that he was, at long last, shaping up? The snake incident could have turned into a goddamn mess but Skeeter had handled it beautifully. She was proud of him. She couldn't wait to tell Tone. She'd call from Washington.

"Did you see that kid with that disgusting snake?" Carrie Hill asked. "I can't believe they let a thing like that on the Metroliner. Think I'll complain."

"Why do you want to complain? What did the snake do to you?"

"It isn't what it did; it's what it could do."

"It's harmless. It's a boa constrictor. They never strike if they're not hungry. And they only strike to kill food. You and I are much too big."

"Ugh. How do you know so much about snakes?"

"I live with Doctor Watson," Christy said beaming. "He's really quite interesting." Good God, was that really her voice calling that hideous creature interesting?

Skeeter held Doctor Watson toward Christy in triumph. Carrie Hill shrank back.

"I think you should fasten his seat belt, Skeets," Christy said with a wink. "Here comes a conductor."

Who cared anymore that Skeeter had blown the door off the chemistry professor's house with a bomb he'd made in class? That he'd been arrested for making a U-turn at 85 M.P.H. in the middle of Rodeo Drive in Tone's Mercedes? That he, with Ed Kurtz in tow, had painted over every number on every door in their apartment building, and replaced it with a wrong one? She'd never loved him more.

As the train began to slow for the station, Carrie Hill extended her hand to Christy. "It's been very good meeting someone who lives with a boa constrictor. I think I should take up something wild like sky diving or hot air ballooning. What do you think?"

Christy laughed.

"I think going to the opera would be a lot safer. And a lot more fun."

Ten

Dulles International Airport

"WHAT DO you mean, 'The Concorde doesn't fly to L.A.'?" Bette Farmington demanded of an exhausted British Airways clerk.

"The Concorde, madam, flies on an intercontinental route. That means it does not fly transcontinental. It flies from New York and Washington to London and from London to New York and Washington."

"I know very well what intercontinental means," Bette snapped, her eyes as empty as Ian's stomach. "Isn't there something we can fly to Los Angeles?"

"Yes, madam. All you need are tickets." Or a broom, he thought. What an airhead. He felt sorry for the good-looking man with her.

"Come on, Bette, I'll arrange for the tickets."

"What time is it? I feel like I've been up all night."

"It's only nine-thirty, Bette. If we're lucky, we'll be in Los Angeles by two or three in the morning."

"I don't know if I feel like a birthday party. Do you? Tone is such a jerk." She grinned. "How about a few more games?"

Good God, the woman was as insatiable for backgammon as she was in bed. He couldn't take too much more of this.

"Let's get the tickets first. The blizzard is making things pretty jammed up here. It looks like a Crimean War bivouac."

Bette laughed. "And most of them are senior citizens. Where did they all come from?"

"I don't know where they came from, Bette, but believe it or not, there are more senior citizens in the United States than the entire population of Canada."

"Now how on earth did you know that?"

"I read a lot. Why don't you sit here while I go find TWA or Eastern or somebody?"

"I think I'll look around for the Ionosphere Club, OK?"

What if it weren't OK? What was he supposed to say? He decided to to smile. His ex-wife Jill used to say that smiling could be a whole way of life. Which reminded him—compared to Jill, Bette had Cuisinart blades in her cunt.

As he headed off toward the shortest lines, Ian saw a tall, sloppy boy with an enormous camera case walk over to Bette and start talking. Probably lost. If I were lost, Ian thought, I'd rather talk to the Gestapo.

Suddenly Bette threw her arms around the kid. She was grinning like she'd just eaten a crib of corn. He heard her yelp, "Skeeter darling. What a surprise. I was hoping I'd get to see you before we all got to L.A."

"It's great to see you, Be...Mom." Funny, Ian thought. He didn't look like he thought it was so great. "Did you just get here?"

"Right, darling. Just in from London."

"Over there rolling up a storm, huh?" Skeeter liked backgammon but avoided playing with his mother. If she didn't win five games out of six, she sulked.

"Speaking of storms, how's little old New York? It must be some mess, what?" Bette spoke American in

London and used Britishisms in New York. "How's school?"

He was about to say "dumb," but stopped himself. Lying was safer. "It's great."

"Are you finding yourself?"

What the fuck was *that* supposed to mean? As far as he knew he'd never been lost.

"Finding myself?"

"Well, I haven't heard from you in months. Your father hasn't told me of any of your escapades. And Christy...well, you know Christy better than I."

"Look, Bette, can't we leave Christy out of this?"

"Certainly, dear. Certainly. Goodness, we are cranky today, what? Can I at least ask where the darling girl is?" Bette scanned the room, her right hand above her eyes. "I don't seem to see her."

"She's somewhere with Antonia and Ed."

"Ed? Do I know Ed? Is he a friend of Christy's?" Her voice dripped innuendo.

"Ed is my friend. My *best* friend. He lives in our building."

How could Tone ever have loved Bette? He must have been nuts or drunk or something.

"Oh. Well, Skeets, have you been figuring out what you're going to be when you grow up?"

What he was going to be when he grew up? Maybe she hadn't noticed, but he was grown up. He was six-feet-two and wore a forty-one long.

"Mother, I consider that a du...an *absurd* question." Gently, he lowered his camera case to the floor. "I'm almost seventeen. Remember?"

Bette stared.

"These days, unlike at the turn of the century when the average life-span was somewhere around forty-five, people my age have a pretty good chance of living to be one hundred. Barring plane crashes, drunken driving fatalities, or ground glass administered by family members. Right?"

"I guess so. I had no idea..." Bette paused. Maybe Skeeter had stopped reading those trashy comics.

"So, how can I possibly tell you what I'm going to do for the next eighty-three years or so? I may go into several fields. See what I mean?"

She heard what he'd said but she wasn't sure she saw what he was getting at. What kinds of fields?

"Put it this way, Bette, what did you want to be when you were seventeen? A teacher? A nurse? An actress?"

"President of the United States."

"Oh, come *on.*"

"OK, Skeeter, I wanted to be a wife and mother. That's what most girls wanted in those days."

"Did you get bored or what?"

"I didn't get bored; your father did. He was fooling around with everyone in his office. He embarrassed me to pieces."

The idea of Bette Farmington being embarrassed by anything was too much for him to swallow. Dad playing the stud. Skeeter laughed.

"Come on, Mom. What *really* happened?"

"You mean your father never told you?"

Tone had said that Bette had taken up backgammon with such a vengeance that she'd pushed them to the brink of bankruptcy. Probably an exaggeration. That she'd refused to have dinner parties or invite his clients for cocktails. That the house was a mess because every maid and cook he'd ever hired quit after two weeks of Bette's drunken gambling parties. Questionable. Tone had met Christy at Juneau Lamb's apartment when Juneau was one of his clients.

"Not exactly, Mom." She seemed pretty agitated. Why

104

make it worse? "Tone and I really don't talk about it."

"What about Christy? Does *she* ever talk about it?"

"All Christy ever talks about is *Allure*." That ought to put the conversation on safer ground.

"That awful magazine? I don't know how she can work there. It's dreadful. Do you ever read it, Skeets?"

"I'm not exactly the target audience, Bette," he laughed. Where was Ed? Where was Antonia? Where was Christy?

"'How cellulite ruined my sex life' by anonymous."

"They never had an article like that in *Allure*."

"Ah-ha, I thought you said you didn't read it?"

"I read Christy's articles. I think they're good. Damn good. I don't care how lousy you are about Christy, Mom, you've got to admit that she's a terrific writer."

"I have to admit no such thing. Nobody ever got a Nobel Prize for writing about fat legs."

Why was it that every single time he tried to talk to his mother, they managed to lock horns within five minutes? Skeeter used to think it was his fault. Well, goddamnitall, it *wasn't* his fault. She had her fangs out for blood. Not seeing her for eight months had done wonders for his perspective.

"That's not the point, Mom, and you know it."

"That's not the point. That's not the point. Well, my boy, what exactly *is* the point? I thought you were growing up. Finally. I guess I was wrong."

The camera case at Skeeter's feet gave a half-hearted little jump. Bette didn't seem to notice.

"I'm sorry, Skeeter. I guess I'm just...tired from the flight. Coming here to Dulles. And Heaven only knows when we'll take off for the Coast. You understand."

He understood, all right. He understood that if he had to put up with Bette and her bad temper and whoever that guy was she was with who looked like an

105

even bigger nerd than Marcy Kurtz's gigolo, he just might get on the next Metroliner back to New York. Metroliner, shit. Greyhound bus. The camera case gave another lurch. Skeeter picked it up and carefully slung it over his shoulder.

"My, you have a lot of camera equipment, darling. Going to get some great shots of the birthday party?"

"I hope so," he said, his lips forming a smile. Could you smile without showing your teeth? For weeks he'd been trying to perfect the look.

"Are you going to be a photographer when you grow up?" Jesus, would she ever stop? Dr. Watson was getting restless.

"No, I don't think so. Overcrowded field. I'm interested in herpetology, though."

Bette looked aghast. "Skeeter! I expected much greater things from you."

Good. Keep expecting. No wonder Tone had married Christy. Suddenly, he felt very protective of Christy. Where was she?

"I just can't believe it. My own son interested in people with sexual organs of both male and female on the same body."

Was she serious? How could anybody confuse hermaphrodites with the study of reptiles and amphibians? One last time he'd be patient. If it killed him.

"Herpetology is a branch of zoology, Mom."

"Marvelous. *Animals* with two sets of genitalia."

That was it. He'd had it. "Listen, I'd love to talk some more, but I've got to find Antonia. She gets lost in crowds." Antonia had never been lost in a crowd in her life but he knew she'd forgive him.

"Maybe we can all have dinner. I'd like you to meet Mr. Harrington. Ian Harrington. He's a sensational backgammon player. One of the greats."

106

"Well, I don't know. There's Christy and Antonia and Ed. And I'm supposed to be rounding up some tickets." The camera case flopped.

"Skeeter, your camera case. It looked like it moved."

"Oh. That's only Doctor Watson."

"What's Doctor Watson?"

"I used to have Sherlock Holmes, too, but I gave him to the zoo. That leaves Doctor Watson. See?"

All Bette saw was an inanimate camera case that seemed to be animating before her eyes.

"What exactly *is* Doctor Watson, Skeeter?" Already she feared the worst—Skeeter wasn't Tone's son for nothing.

"Actually, he's a…boa…constrictor, Mom."

"A *snake*? In there?" She aimed a shiny red nail at the camera case.

"That's what herpetology is, Mom."

"Oh, that." Bette laughed gaily. "I just made that up about…the hermaphrodites, darling." Thank God. She'd thought it was the study of herpes.

"Gotta go, Mom. See you later." He bent down and kissed her. She smelled like damp sawdust. Or camel's feet. "I'm looking forward to meeting Mr. Harrington."

He shouldn't go into zoology; he should be a career diplomat.

ELEVEN

New York City

TONE SLAMMED the front door. "I'm home from the Coast."

It was ominously quiet. "Christy?" His voice echoed down the hall.

People crossing the country in prairie schooners had had it better, Tone was convinced. What was an Indian raid or two compared to the red eye from L.A. to D.C.?

And where in hell was Christy? The kids? He dropped his package from Giorgio's on the green marble foyer console.

He needed a drink. Or coffee. Or scrambled eggs. *Some*thing. He settled for a vodka and Diet Coke.

What time was it? The kitchen clock had stopped somewhere around six. His watch had stopped at 3:30. He felt fifty, all right. A hundred was more like it.

"Happy birthday, swinger," he said to the empty room.

As he prowled through the apartment, he realized that he hadn't anticipated how long two years would feel. Everything looked so much smaller, the way it did when you came home from college or a long trip to Europe.

The white rug in the living room looked like a 19th-century map of the Austro-Hungarian Empire, done in various shades of red.

Christy's favorite chair was broken. What the hell had happened here? She'd loved that chair when she'd bought it at Mallet's, in London. Its mate was in the Brighton Pavillion.

He wandered into Skeeter's room. Exactly the same. A grade B 1950 sci-fi movie set. He quickly closed the door.

Antonia's room. Silver mylar tented her canopy bed. A life-size poster of Louis Jourdan. Dracula gazing at him with red eyes. No more David Cassidy, at least.

Their room. He looked around for something—anything—familiar. The old Tone Shaw smiled at him from a Tiffany frame on Christy's bed-table. Captain Corporate. Pinstripes. Red tie. White shirt. Eyes with the sparkle of a dead light bulb.

He got up and opened the door to his closet. The bracing scent of moth balls. Everything in garment bags. His New York existence, neatly tagged.

He slammed the door, picked up the phone and dialed the super. Seven rings. No answer. The bedroom clock said 10:55.

He started turning on the lights. The place was a goddamn morgue. Dank. Cheerless as a Dickens counting house.

The front doorbell rang. He ran into the hallway. "Christy?"

Santo, the afternoon doorman, not yet in uniform, stood in the outside foyer, a Mafia funeral bouquet cradled in his huge arms.

Tone opened the door.

"Flowers for Mrs. Shaw." Santo didn't recognize him.

Tone's heart pounded. He took a dollar bill out of his pocket and handed it to Santo, who still didn't seem to recognize him.

How many strange men had Christy had in their apartment?

Tone began to quake with rage.

He dumped the flowers on the table next to the perfume and scented candles he'd brought for Christy from Giorgios. Giorgios was so exclusive, they used an "unlisted" toll-free telephone number on their yellow-and-white striped, crested stationery. That was Rodeo Drive for you.

There was a card with the flowers. So what. Most flowers came with cards.

Should he read it? It wasn't addressed to him. He really shouldn't open it. But Christy wasn't there. He could pretend that someone else opened it; that it had been opened by mistake. Shit. It was his apartment. Christy was his wife. He snatched the little envelope and ripped it open.

I'll treasure last night's memories for a lifetime,
Flemming, the Bastard of Belgrave Square.

What the fuck was that supposed to mean? What kinds of memories deserved ten pounds of tulips, fresias, wild orchids and gardenias?

Tone picked up Christy's present and threw it as hard as he could into the living room. The package exploded. Perfume splattered the lamps and sofa. The scented candle wound up in the fireplace. $287 shot to hell.

He wrenched open the front door and headed for the elevator. He was going to get to the bottom of this once and for all.

He didn't hear the telephone ringing.

———————————

After a frozen walk around the block, Tone stormed back to the apartment. He sure as hell wasn't going to find Christy out in the street. At least he'd cooled off. He'd forgotten just how cold it gets in New York with that stiff, icy wind from the East River.

First he'd call *Allure*. It was Friday. Seemed like Saturday, or like it should be Saturday. Like he'd left Beverly Hills months ago.

Juneau Lamb would know where Christy was. What if she was away on one of her goddamn beauty trips? Ed Kurtz's mother. What *was* her name? Christ. Down in 12-C. Mary? Merry? Martina? Shit. Marty. That was it. Good old Marty would know where the kids were. The schools had to be closed. Maybe the Tutoring School was open.

Maybe he should call the cops.

"Hello? Nineteenth precinct? I want to report a missing wife and two kids. Well, they're not kids exactly. One is eight. (Or is Antonia nine?) And the boy is seventeen. No, I don't know what they were wearing. I haven't seen them in...oh, three or four months. My wife?

"Well, she's very pretty. Has blue eyes and black hair. It's curly. She's on the thin side. I don't know. One-ten, maybe. About five-feet-five. I'm not sure what she was wearing. Slacks probably. I don't know. I haven't seen her since last Sunday afternoon when she was wearing a white linen pants suit and an Yves St. Laurent scarf."

They'd arrest *him*. Or send him to Bellevue to sober up.

A tall, blond man in a British overcoat was talking to Santo. Maybe this time Santo would recognize him. He'd be damned if he'd introduce himself to his own doorman. But then why shouldn't he? How many people did Santo see every day? And how many times had Santo seen him lately? Not even once in the past two years.

"Are you sure you haven't seen Mrs. Shaw this morning?" the blond man asked.

112

"No, sir. I took the flowers up. I told you that. No Mrs. Shaw. She probably went to California, *señor*."

"But she couldn't have gone to California. The airports are closed. The snow."

"I wouldn't know, *señor*. I don't fly since I came here fifteen years ago."

Tone took the bullshit by the horns and walked right up to the blond man.

"Flemming?"

The man turned, hesitating. "Yes?"

"Hiya. I'm Tone Shaw." Tone extended his hand, remembering what a handshake had done for his friendship with Jake Witt. Had that been only yesterday?

At once Flemming understood. *Her* husband. He was here. From Beverly Hills. He'd found the flowers. That stupid note. Christ.

"Can't tell you how much I like 'Beverly Hills Babe,'" Flemming said with as much honesty as he could muster. Well, he *did* like it.

Tone smiled. "Great, fella. I'm glad. It's one of my favorites."

How could he ask this guy where Christy was? Santo said she'd probably gone to California. Had they passed on the Metroliner? In the not-so-friendly skies?

Could they have both had the same idea?

But when had she left for Washington? And what was all this about those memories of last night? Tone felt like introducing Flemming to Jake Witt. They deserved each other. Nobody that good looking could be straight. He hoped. He prayed.

"About the flowers, Mr. Shaw," Flemming said. "You see, I had an interview with Mrs. Shaw yesterday. I'm going to work for *Allure*."

"Oh." So that was it. "They're doing a section on men?" That wasn't like that asshole Doran. On second thought,

113

if it would sell magazines, Doran would put orangutans mating in the trees in the center spread.

Flemming thought he'd let that go by. "Are you here for long, Mr. Shaw?"

"Tone. Tone. I'm not sure. Listen, do you want to come up for coffee or something? Too damn cold down here. I've got West Coast thin blood." He *was* shivering. And anyway he didn't want to have a conversation about Christy in front of the doorman. Things were sticky enough.

When they got off the elevator, Flemming hesitated, not knowing whether to go to the left or the right.

Great, thought Tone. He's never been up here before. Or else he's a method actor.

"How about a Bloody Mary?"

Flemming nodded, unbuttoning the coat. Underneath, he was wearing jeans and a Japanese sweater.

"I'll level with you, Flem." You couldn't call someone Flem. "When was the last time you saw Christy?"

"After my interview yesterday, at *Allure*, we had a drink to celebrate my new job. Mrs. Shaw said she was going to fly to the Coast and take her children. That it was your birthday. There was a big party. She was upset that the blizzard had closed the airports. That's about it," he said, his eyes wandering from the flower arrangement to the broken perfume bottles in the living room. He'd gone overboard with the flowers. But how the hell was he supposed to know Tone Shaw would show up?

Screw the coffee.

Tone mixed two Bloodies and handed one to Flemming. "Did you meet Juneau Lamb at *Allure*?"

"No. She'd left for the day."

"Reed Doran?"

"Reed Doran?"

"The publisher?"

114

"No. Actually, no one was there except Mrs. Shaw. The offices were closed because of the snow. She was waiting because she hadn't been able to reach me by phone."

"I think I'll give Juneau Lamb a call," Tone headed back to the kitchen. Why did people put phones in the kitchen? In Beverly Hills that was the one place he didn't have a phone.

"I must go, Mr. Shaw. I hope Mrs. Shaw...well, I'm sure you'll find her. I know how much she was looking foward to going." Flemming picked up his coat and crossed to the front door in three strides. "Good luck."

Let's keep out of touch, Tone thought, as he heard the door close.

Juneau Lamb.

Tone liked Juneau Lamb.

When he'd first met her, that spring afternoon so many years ago—it must be fifteen? sixteen years ago?—she was so vulnerable and sad. When she'd finished her story, he'd assigned the case to one of the best junior partners.

Fourteen years before, she'd had a child—a daughter. The child had been left with a family on a small farm in Massachusetts or someplace. It wasn't the kind of case he liked to handle and apparently they hadn't been able to come up with anything. The foster parents were killed or disappeared. The child vanished. Juneau finally gave up.

A man answered Juneau's phone.

"Is Juneau Lamb at home? This is Tone Shaw—Christy Shaw's husband—speaking."

There was some whispering in the background before Juneau got on the line.

"Tone. How are you?"

"Just fine." What was he saying? "I'm trying to track

Christy down. No one seems to know where she is and I'm worried about her. And the kids. They've all disappeared."

"Last time I spoke to her she was on her way to California."

"But the airports are closed."

"Oh." There was a long silence. "I didn't know."

A magazine editor who didn't read the papers? Listen to the radio? Watch television?

"I've been tied up, Tone. I wasn't in the office yesterday to speak of. Well, I guess you might as well be the first to know: I'm getting married. And I'm leaving *Allure*. I wish Christy were there with you so I could tell her. You know, of course, what this means?"

He knew. It meant that his worst fears were about to be confirmed. Christy was going to become editor-in-chief. She'd be so busy she'd never get to Beverly Hills again. Shit.

"That's great, Juneau. Just great. Who's the lucky man?"

"Why, Reed Doran. The publisher of *Allure*. Nothing like a little nepotism, we always say."

"Well, congratulations to you both. And if you should hear from Christy, ask her to call me. I'm in New York."

He called Rodeo Drive. Michele Quinton answered.

"Well, lover, we're all ready for the big day and where's the big boy?"

"Michele, my love, are Christy and the kids there?"

"Christy and the kids? I don't see them, do you see Christy and the kids, Jake?" Christ, she was going into her hyena imitation. That meant she was stoned. At nine o'clock in the morning. They probably hadn't been to bed.

"Who's there, Michele?"

"Your class. All ten of them. With some friends. Miranda whosis. She got a part, Tone."

116

"Put her on, Michele."

"I can't. She's celebrating."

"Can't she talk and celebrate at the same time?"

"I don't think so. Her speaking apparatus is otherwise engaged."

"What's the part?"

"Olivia? Olympia? Ophelia?"

"Oblivia," Tone said and hung up.

They weren't at Rodeo Drive. They weren't at 72nd and Park. They weren't at *Allure*. Where in God's name were they?

Marcy Kurtz would know. Tone dashed out to the elevator and descended to the twelfth floor. He leaned on the buzzer. It played the first four notes of Beethoven's Fifth. How had the building allowed *that*?

Marcy's "friend" answered the door. Tone could never remember the guy's name. Something basic, no frills. Fred? Damn. Frank. That was it. Frank. Tone followed him into the living room. The guy's walk had been choreographed by a Kremlinologist.

"Marcy, darling, Tone Shaw is here." He turned. "How about a drink? My immortal soul tells me it's Bloody Mary time. Or would you care for something else? A Mimosa? Bullshot? Bloody Bull? White wine?"

Tone longed to do his Bela Lugosi imitation, "Ho-ho, Van Helsing, I seldom drink vine," but he restrained himself. Poor Frank was trying to be cordial. He desperately needed an acting lesson. Less strut and more bounce.

"A Bloody Mary would be just great. Thanks. I think jet lag is beginning to do its magic."

Frank laughed and disappeared.

Marty—no, damnit, *Marcy*, loomed into view. She shook hands as though she were about to Indian wrestle. "Well, Tone. You're the last person I expected to see. Why aren't you in California?"

"Because I'm here, Marcy. How are you?"

Frank appeared with the Bloody Marys. Tone thanked him and drank a mouthful. Very good. The guy had talent.

"Well, Tone, you know where Christy and the kids are, don't you?"

If I knew that, O oracle, would I be sitting here on your B. Altman French Provincial sofa?

"I know they were coming to Los Angeles and then the blizzard closed the airports. I flew to Dulles, took the Metroliner up. I thought everyone would be *here*, Marcy."

"Your Skeeter got the brilliant idea of doing just that. In reverse, of course. Did you call your house?"

"Not there."

"How about Dulles? Did you try there?"

"The circuits are all busy."

"They're probably about to land right now. If you want to have a birthday party with them, you'd better retrace your steps." Marcy started laughing.

What was it with everyone laughing this morning? They were all high or drunk, laughing and giggling. Well, he, for one, didn't feel like laughing.

"Ships that pass in the night, Tone. Remember the last line of *The Great Gatsby*? Ships that pass in the night, I tell you." She slapped her knee. Her bracelets clanked.

Tone remembered the last line of *The Great Gatsby* a lot better than Marcy Kurtz. It seemed to him that she was a "boat against the current, borne back ceaselessly into the past." If he'd been casting her in a play, only eye of newt and toe of frog came to mind as lines suitable for her utterance.

TWELVE

Washington, D.C.

THERE WERE only three first class seats left. That meant Christy, Skeeter and Ed could get on a flight. Or, Ed, Skeeter and Antonia. Or, or, or.

"Let's draw straws," said Ed.

"Yeah, and the loser gets thrown out of the life raft to the sharks so the survivors can save on drinking water."

Christy had never been so tired. Ed couldn't fly alone. He'd never been to L.A. before. He'd probably get lost. Antonia was too young. It didn't seem fair to separate Skeeter from his best friend.

"OK, this is *it*," Christy announced. "The three of you will go and I'll follow on the very next flight."

"But Mother," Antonia pressed her head against Christy's shoulder, "the next flight may not be till tomorrow."

"What's tomorrow when you already have Amtrak lag?" Ed observed.

He was right, thought Christy. She glanced at her watch. A little after midnight. She was past the point of caring.

"Really, gang. It's the way to do it. Skeeter is in charge, Antonia. Ed."

"OK." They picked up their bags and she handed them the tickets.

"See you on Rodeo Drive. We'll have a great time tomorrow. It'll be as though this never happened."

"I don't mind this. It beats du...many things I could name but don't choose to." Skeeter kissed Christy's cheek. Ed kissed her other cheek and Antonia threw herself into Christy's arms.

Skeeter hadn't mentioned Bette to Christy. He figured she had enough to deal with. Anyway, Bette had probably gotten on a plane by now.

"Ian, if you don't massage the back of my neck, I think my head is going to come off," Bette moaned. "When is that goddamn stinking plane going to take off, anyhow?"

"They're refueling right now, Bette. It shouldn't be too long."

"Everything's too long when you're not having fun."

"How about some aspirin? It might help you snooze off."

"I've got a pound of codeine in my bag, sweets. Besides, if I snooze off, I won't be able to play any more."

At this point Ian didn't think he'd be able to see the dice. If he lost any more, he'd be her indentured slave for life.

Christy stared into space. How much longer? One could stand almost anything as long as it was finite.

Just as she was opening a copy of *Vogue* she heard them calling her flight.

How had she managed to get on a flight ahead of the kids?

As she sat in her seat and listened to the engines warming up, the bells in the cabin, and the static preceding the captain's inevitable announcements, she felt her palms getting moist. It was always like this...

Several years ago on a flight to London, she'd had the scare of her life. As the plane moved out over the Atlantic, it suddenly went into a nose dive. Everything in the kitchens had clattered to the floor. The attendants were ordered to their seats. The no smoking and fasten seat belt signs flashed like ambulance lights.

The plane had been heading straight for the ocean when suddenly it stopped, suspended, and then slowly it began to climb.

Christy's first thought had been: why couldn't this have happened on the way back from Paris rather than on the way over to London?

For eight years, on every single one of her numerous flights, she resuffered that three minutes.

Tonight was no exception. Her small, cold, wet hands gripped the arms of the seat. Her feet were planted so firmly that her heels dug tiny holes in the carpet.

The man next to the window patted her hand. "First time up? Well, you'll be just fine once they get the bar cart rolling in the aisles."

Christy smiled weakly and turned her head away from the window.

Somewhere behind and below, there was a cataclysmic explosion. It sounded like a bomb. Christy had only heard bombs in the movies but that's what it sounded like. The plane vibrated. There was a series of small explosions.

Everyone was trying to get to a window. The sky flared briefly red, orange, pink before they soared into the clouds.

The crackle. The captain was speaking.

"Seems they've had some trouble at Dulles. It's too soon to tell exactly what's going on. Some kind of fire. We don't know what caused it. We'll keep you informed as soon as we know anything."

As quickly as Christy blotted them, fresh, hot tears poured down her face. Those kids. Alone. How could she have deserted them? She pressed the call button.

An attendant appeared beside her. "Please tell me what happened. My children are back there."

"It's a fire on one of the runways. That's all we know right now, ma'am. Can I get you something?"

"Fire on the runway? Not in the terminal?"

"No. Outside. Definitely."

Christy mumbled a thank you. She'd had it. If the kids get out of this, she'd move to California. Forget *Allure*.

She wished she had her portable tape recorder. This was one tape Tone would love to replay.

Frank burst into the living room. "Quick. Come and see what's on the news."

Marcy and Tone ran into her library where Channel 2 was reporting what looked like the grim spectacle of a jumbo jet that had crashed on take-off at Dulles International Airport.

"Wow," said Ed as the hostess placed his hot snack on the little tray in front of him, "this is my first meal on a 747."

"And it may be your last," said Skeeter. "Only the High Lama knows for sure where or when this food came into being. It's probably been frozen since the second Ice Age. Maybe the first."

122

"I happen to adore ham-and-cheese. Velveeta from the gourmet department. Think we can get a beer?"

"Sure. Being that they're probably fresh out of *Chateau Mouton Rothschild.*"

"Oh, Christ. Don't remind me," sighed Ed. "Your white carpet and your white sofa."

"And the Regency chair which looks like it's been through an automobile compactor. Lucky for you, Edmundo, I think we can arrange an out-of-court settlement."

"I don't see how you gibbering goons can eat *any*thing," Antonia snapped, "after that horrible thing at the airport."

"Horrible, my ass. One of life's little traumas." Skeeter yawned and bit into his sandwich.

"Skeeter, shut up," Antonia's eyes were glazed with tears. "We don't even know where Mother is."

"Come on, Antonia, Christy is OK. She took off before we did. You know that."

"How do I know that?"

"She was on her way to the gate when we were boarding."

"Are you sure? Are you absolutely sure, Skeeter?"

"Sure. Besides, the captain said it was only an explosion."

"Enola Gay created an explosion," Ed added, between sips of his beer. "Think they have any imported ketchup?"

"Ch-rist, people, it was a fire in an empty plane. No one was hurt. The runway's open by now. Eat your cuisine before it crawls away."

Sullenly, Antonia chewed her sandwich. Why couldn't Daddy ever come to New York? Why was it always Mother who had to catch a plane? Mother who had jet lag? Mother who was so exhausted at the end of the day she could barely stay awake through dinner? Daddy hadn't been home in a year. No, two years. On his forty-eighth birthday. Tomorrow he'd be fifty.

"Skeeter," Antonia asked, "are you going to be like Daddy when you grow up?"

"What is that supposed to mean?"

"You know. Go to law school. Go into business. Create. Be like Daddy."

"Antonia means do you have any intentions of becoming a tycoon in your spare time," Ed offered.

"A tycoon? You mean an over-achiever, over-reacher, over-killer masquerading as lawyer, writer, producer and bullshit artist? Maybe yes. Maybe no. According to Mrs. Potswell, my history teacher, I'm already exhibiting some of the signs."

"Your history teacher? Ah, yes at the Tutoring School. The last refuge of the pot-smoking, glue-sniffing, coke-snorting East Side preppie dropout and fuck-up." Ed pushed the call button.

"Shit, Kurtz, you certainly know how to talk in hyphenated words," Skeeter said sourly. "You're just jealous because you get such good grades at Andover. Tutoring wouldn't touch you with a ten-foot dildo."

" *There are more things in heaven and earth, Horatio, than are dreamt of in your philosophy.'* Among them, ten-foot dildoes."

"Hamlet, Act One, scene five," Skeeter replied. "I'm making no decisions until I'm sure of what I'm in for."

"You never know what you're in for until it's too late. Just look at my mother and Prince Disarming." Ed grinned with demonic satisfaction.

"We should all be planning for the future, if we had brains." Antonia had apparently recovered.

Skeeter rolled his eyes. Who needed philosophy from Antonia?

"Suppose the worst had happened. Suppose Mother

124

had been in that plane and it hadn't just been a fire but a real crash. You know...suppose she hadn't made it to take off? What would she be doing now?"

"Flying to California to live with Tone," Skeeter said, matter-of-factly, his voice even and calm. All they needed now was Antonia sobbing for five hours.

She almost smiled. "You know anxiety always triggers my imagination. The *worst* parts of my imagination."

Ed scratched his stomach, anxious to change the direction of the conversation. "Wish to hell we could sneak a joint in the lavatory."

"No smoking in there. Ever. That's how planes blow up. And besides, I think we've had enough explosions for one enchanted evening," Antonia said tightly. "Besides, you boys should give up on joints."

Ed drew back in mock horror.

"One of the greatest pleasures in life, Antonia? Why?"

"As everyone knows, marijuana smoke is more irritating than tobacco smoke. Not that I'm recommending cigarettes. It has a higher tar content, too. And it gives you chronic bronchitis and emphysema."

Skeeter laughed.

"Oh, shove it, Antonia."

"Since when are you a graduate of Harvard Medical?" Ed pushed his call button again. "Think I'll indulge in another liver-fracturing beer. Care to join me?"

"You'll be sorry," Antonia said. "Just wait until all those contaminating chemicals, bacteria and...ugh... fungus course through your systems."

"What chemicals?"

"Paraquet, for example. It's an insecticide that can blitz your lungs."

Skeeter yawned.

"Great. Terrific. I haven't had my lungs blitzed in many moons."

"Pot can give you salmonella."

"I thought you got salmonella from contaminated tuna or eating out of opened tin cans, Ant."

"Call me Ant, I'll call you Skeets. Just wait until you both come down with aspergillus. You'll sing a different tune."

"Sing a different tune—that's my mother's favorite line. After thirty years of television—from "I Love Lucy" to the Moral Majority, it's about the only thing she can think of to say to me. She doesn't even tell me to pick up my feet any more," Ed said, grinning.

"Pick up your feet," Skeeter laughed. "Do you know how utterly ridiculous that image is?"

"Ridiculous?"

"How does one go about picking up his feet? It's like that joke about the Polish disco."

Antonia groaned. "Must we?"

"What's the Polish disco?" Ed asked, rubbing his eyes.

Skeeter jumped into the aisle. First, he grabbed his left leg, lifted it with both hands and dropped his foot to the floor. Then, he repeated the procedure with his right leg.

"Dis go here and dis go dere." He dissolved. "Get it gang? Dis go—disco?"

Ed stared.

"Ch-rist, will that lay 'em end to end on Rodeo Drive. So suave. Listen, I don't know about you Shaws but I'm going to sleep. I feel like I've just done the Australian crawl to Sydney and back."

———————

For the first time since she hauled herself out of bed that morning, Christy began to relax.

The plane at Dulles had been empty. The fire was out. No one had been hurt. The kids, clearly, hadn't been anywhere near it. Still, she felt the aftereffects of

126

the scare. She opened her attaché and took out a pad and pen.

The last thing in the world she felt like doing was working. She stifled a yawn and forced herself.

"The image of beauty in America is moving forward with the baby boom. In 1981, not one *Allure* model was under thirty; today many models are forty and over.

"The glorious Linda Evans of the popular TV series "Dynasty" was voted in several polls the most beautiful woman in America in 1983. Linda is forty."

The words swam on the paper but Christy continued. The important thing was to get it all down. She could edit later.

"Forty-year-old women have always been beautiful but until now, no one wanted to admit it because the shift was to youth. For the first time in history, the young population is shrinking; less and less attention is being paid to kids." Christy paused. Should she use the word "kids"?

She was too tired for this.

Oh, Tone, where are you? Out with one of those luscious young women that no one is paying any attention to anymore? What's going to happen to us? Maybe it's already happened. She shook her head. Maybe she should sleep. But she had to finish the article before she got to Beverly Hills. There would be no time to work over the weekend. Not with the party and the kids. There was plenty of time to sleep on her way back to New York.

She turned her attention back to "Age Before Beauty—a Fresh-Faced Look." Another two thousand words. Gasp.

Why was sixty-five the age of retirement? She rifled through her notes. Ah. That's when Bismarck decided that his captains should retire.

127

It made about as much sense as anything. What about the generals? When did they retire? The majors? What other ranks were there in an army? She'd ask Tone. His fund of trivia was unparalleled.

To hell with Prince Otto von Bismarck. The Iron Chancellor couldn't help her deal with the baby boom. She was the perfect example of a baby boomer. Twenty-five percent had no children; another twenty-five percent had one child. Christy Shaw, overachieving baby boomer and mother of one.

She'd thought of having another child, but there never seemed to be enough time. Having Skeeter around was like having ten children. In a way, that girl on the train— what was her name? Carrie Hill. Carrie had been right. Christy had even less time than Carrie. Face it, Christy. You're doing what you wanted. Super careerwoman. Supermom. Super wife. Ha. Superwoman.

"Christy, business is all you ever think about," Juneau had told her one ugly, nervous morning.

It's a damn good thing, too, Juneau darling, Christy had ached to reply. But she'd bitten her tongue. Damn it, business was *not* the only thing she thought about. She thought about Tone more than anything, more than anyone.

And she shared her life with him, mostly on his terms.

At first, right after they married, Christy had felt helpless around him.

"After all, Tone *is* old enough to be your father," Juneau had said often enough. But he wasn't her father.

Who was? She was sinking into one of her depressions.

She walked haltingly to the lavatory, clutching at the backs of the seats. There was a lot of turbulence tonight. Or this morning. Or whenever the hell it was.

A pale, drawn face with milky blue circles underlining giant eyes stared back at her from the mirror in the dim, tiny room.

Must be all the stress. Last month, she'd done an article on New York and Los Angeles, the two most stressful cities in the United States. She had the luck to live in *both* of them. She splashed water in her stranger's face and stroked on a ribbon of bright pink lipstick. The contrast made her look older, tireder, paler.

"Beauty secrets, hah," Christy said to the mirror. The people who lived the longest were the people who were having a good time. Was she having a good time?

"Well, Christy, you packed your lunch box." The bleak image in the mirror stared back.

THIRTEEN

New York City

WHY COULDN'T the people who worked for the airlines speak English? Tone was fuming.

"You don't know when the airport will open? No, I know you're not a weatherman, madam. I *know* you're not a madam, either. Thank you."

Back to D.C., back to Dulles, back to L.A. At the rate he was going, he'd make it back to Rodeo Drive in time for Easter.

At least he had some information about the crash. It had only been a small fire, not a crash but an explosion. No one had been hurt. Should he believe the TV people? His instincts told him no. He imagined Christy in traction, the kids, comatose, hanging by a thread on life support systems. Stop being counterproductive, he told himself. It was his crazy genes that were responsible for Antonia's outrageous imagination and Skeeter's bizarre antics—that's what Christy always said, anyway.

He slammed down the phone for what seemed like the hundredth time. Stormed to his closet and pulled out an old navy cashmere coat, scarf and gloves. The camphor made his eyes smart.

Did these look like faggot clothes? Maybe that's what

had turned on Jake Witt. But he hadn't been wearing any clothes.

Did he look like a pansy? Talk like one? Bullshit. He had never, not once, in his entire life, given any indication that he was interested in balling a guy.

He stuffed his arms into his sleeves. A little tight. He glanced at himself in the mirror. He did not look like one. Definitely not.

But who could tell any more? Preppy gators were stuck on everything. Men playing polo peeking out from every set of clothed pectorals around.

Before he left for Penn Station, Tone decided to make one last stab. He'd call some Washington hospitals. The only one he could think of off the top of his head was George Washington University Hospital. On impulse, he dialed information and got the number.

They had admitted a Mrs. Shaw. No news on her condition. No one else named Shaw was listed. They weren't sure if she'd been at Dulles. It was too soon to tell anything. Including her first name. It would be better if he came to the hospital.

Goddamn frustrating. Granted, Shaw was a fairly ordinary name. They had said *Mrs.* Shaw. So it wasn't Antonia.

Tone hated it when things were out of his hands. He had a headache. He never got headaches. Bloody Marys with Marcy and what's-his-name. Frank. The guy was as dumb as a shellacked gourd.

In the subway, Tone tried to figure out his next move. He had a couple of hours. He'd work. Keep his mind off Christy.

He had plenty of irons in the fire. His sit-com about a hairdresser called "The Hair House." Sit-Downs, a series of one-minute exercises executives could do at their desks. And his favorite. They even had sponsors for it. A show called "Hot Dogs 'n Peanut Butter," the first cooking show for latchkey kids. It explained how children who came home to an empty house or apartment could fix simple meals for themselves without burning the house down.

Had Antonia ever come home to an empty apartment? Had Christy ever left her alone with a casserole? Or a can of Chunky Soup to heat up? He'd have to ask Christy about that. It would probably be another can of worms. Maybe he should mind his own business. But Antonia *was* his business. His stomach felt like a bag of bricks.

He wanted to do something with a marriage show. About five million people were getting married every year now. Maybe Christy had some ideas. She usually did. What a team they were. If only she would pull with him instead of away from him.

He had tried to be straight with her, to understand her goals. Dammit, marriage was *hard.*

But it had been harder with Bette. Much harder. Bette was a Fifties prom queen. A cliché Southern belle who'd lived the Me Generation twenty years before it overtook America. He had loved her. But he wasn't so sure that she'd loved him. More than attention, that is.

He prayed daily that she would remarry and get off his payroll. Not that she was bankrupting him exactly, but she did extract a hefty $80,000 a year. At this point he'd rather donate it to save the cockroaches.

At Penn Station, he bought a ticket for Amtrak. In three hours, they'd leave for Washington. In another three, they'd be there. Cab to Dulles. Five hours to the Coast. Half hour to the house. Maybe they'd leave some birthday cake for him.

FOURTEEN

Beverly Hills

"AND THE fireplace was dragged over from a 13th-century castle in Chinon, France. Lends an air of *petite manoir,* don't you think?" Skeeter said as he opened his camera case and let Doctor Watson glide forth into the air conditioned living room at 514 North Rodeo Drive. "Do not neglect the coffered, hand-painted ceilings," he swung his arms wide. "And you thought Park Avenue was where it's at."

"I never said that, Skeets," Ed said quickly, looking around. It was some living room.

Statues. Tile. Paved entry. Foyer. Gold walls. Nobody had gold walls. Except maybe Pope Leo X.

"No wonder Christy works so hard at *Manure.* This is great."

Skeeter laughed.

"Christy couldn't pay for the cocktail table, Ed. It all came from my grandfather Shaw, Tone's father. All the way from Park Avenue. If you think this is great, wait until we go shopping."

"Who wants to go shopping? I want to see some sights. Some natives."

"Shopping on Rodeo Drive *is* seeing the sights, Ed.

That's what the natives do. No commie sympathizers in this neighborhood. We'll hit Jerry Magnin's and Hermes. Then we'll take Antonia to lunch at Cafe Pastel."

"Sounds too gay. I want to see some Mexicans and Iranians and go to some Chinese places."

"Je-sus, Ed, we can do *that* in New York. You gotta get the feel of things out here. Everything's beautiful. Outdoors. Speaking of which, let's change and go for a swim. I'm going to call Tone's office. He's probably having an early meeting."

"It's Saturday, stupid," Antonia snapped. "And it's a little past seven o'clock in the morning. He won't be at his office."

"OK, OK, Antonia. Then we'll go for a swim. Get some breakfast. Sooner or later, someone's bound to turn up."

"Like Mother, for example?"

"Shhh," Ed whispered, "did you hear anything?"

"Like what?" Skeeter scanned the room.

"Like a snore."

"Yeah." They followed the sound. Behind a Louis XV needlepoint settee lay Jake Witt, his head propped on a pile of silk pillows. He was naked.

"Whoever he is," Ed noted, "he's bare-assed."

"It's the guy Tone writes songs with. Jake somebody. Sure looks like shit."

"What should we do with him?"

"Why should we do anything with him? He doesn't seem to be unhappy. Probably sleeping off some coke or something."

"Ever try coke, Skeets?"

"No. But I'm broad minded. Got any?"

Ed picked up a jar and a tiny spoon from a draped table. "What do you think?"

A pale Antonia reappeared in the living room. "Skeeter, Ed. Quick. I think something awful has happened."

"What?" Sometimes Antonia could really be a pain.

"Please guys, this is serious. There's a woman in our pool."

"So?"

"I think...she's...dead."

Even at seven in the morning, the L.A. airport was a depressing place. Not as depressing as New York's Port Authority Bus Terminal, maybe—the pervasive odor of urine, sweat, pot and pine cleaner was missing—but it did have many of the same people. Men in short-sleeved shirts. Women in sleeveless dresses. Both cut from the same bolt. All with stomachs, busts, upper arms. Where were the California slim, sun-streaked blonds of the television commercials? In bed with each other?

After what seemed like hours, Christy stepped off the conveyer belt and almost skipped to the exit and a cab.

In less than forty minutes, she was on Rodeo Drive.

Turning onto the Drive was a little like wandering past the unkempt brick tenements and mouldering brownstones of Manhattan's East Twenties to Gramercy Park, with its elegant high fence barring anyone without a gold key; its greenery and benches, its calm timelessness, its statue of Edwin Booth as Hamlet guarding the center walk.

Rodeo Drive had invisible gold keys. Through Tone, she possessed one. At the moment, it didn't seem to be unlocking anything particularly wonderful for her. Where was Tone?

They glided in front of 514 North, a cross between pink Twenties hacienda and Spanish Colonial.

Every house on the Drive was dramatically different, and yet there was a feeling of sameness, perfection, isolation, even with, as Tone loved to say, three-foot zoning. Here, Tudor, Regency, Second Empire mansions snuggled next to Mount Vernon kissing cousins, million-dollar elves cottages and Avenue Foch clones. For all their inhabitants cared, each might have been in the center of a fifty-acre deer park.

This morning, the loudest sound on Rodeo was the insistent, muffled hum of a hundred or so sprinkler systems.

Why was she so hungry? They'd all eaten something on the train, again on the plane. She couldn't remember what. God, for a huge glass of fresh orange juice. The kind they served at the Beverly Hills Hotel. With smoked salmon and scrambled eggs. Rye toast. Steaming coffee. Her stomach was digesting itself. Maybe Tone had something in the fridge besides coffee yogurt and protein bread. She paid the driver, grabbed her Channel 13 bag and scampered up the path. The house looked as though no one lived there.

"Antonia? Skeeter? Ed? Anybody here?"

The temperature was climbing. Heat used to make her feel sexy; now it just knocked her out. Her forehead was already beaded with perspiration. And it had taken just a few seconds to walk up the path from the air-conditioned cab to the air-conditioned house.

"Tone? Anyone here?" If she yelled too loud, she'd be arrested. One night as she and Tone had strolled down Rodeo from the Beverly Hills Hotel, five blocks north, a young policeman had tried to pick them up as a hooker and his pimp. She smiled remembering that night. Things had been a lot more fun then. A lot less complicated.

The kids *must* be here. They'd all taken off within a half hour of each other. "Hey, where is everybody?"

She ambled through the house out to the kitchen and onto the patio, her thoughts returning to Juneau and *Allure*.

She hoped Juneau had managed to get to Miami and taken off for Nevis. If the new sequences on Bikini Beauty weren't shot this week, they were going to miss the deadline.

"Skeeter?" As she moved through the hedge's moon gate aperture she saw him giving mouth-to-mouth resuscitation to a pale and wet young woman. What the hell was going on *now*? Had one of Tone's protégés staggered drunk into the pool?

"What happened?"

"Mother." Antonia threw herself into Christy's arms. "We...found this girl in the pool. I thought it was all over but Skeeter saved her."

Christy peered at the limp body. "It's Mirinda. One of Tone's students." She placed her fingers in the groove on the side of Mirinda's neck. Her pulse was strong. Skeeter stood up. "I think she's OK now."

"Did anyone call an ambulance?"

"Of course, Mother." Antonia was her usual infuriatingly serene self. "I got the boys out here and then *I* called. *I* told them not to turn on any sirens."

Christy suppressed a sigh.

If Antonia weren't her own daughter, she could really dislike her.

"Tell me, what happened."

Ed stepped around the soggy Mirinda.

"Well, Mrs. Shaw, Skeeter was showing me around when Antonia came running in saying that someone was floating in the pool. We ran out here. Then you came out."

Mirinda was squirming and sputtering awake.

"Who're you? Whe—where's Tone?"

I wish I knew, thought Christy. "Just relax, Mirinda. Take a few deep breaths."

Mirinda tried to sit up and slumped back on the aqua/salmon tiles.

"I wish to hell Tone would turn the heat down in the pool. I was fine until I got into the pool. Then I just got really sleepy and—well—I don't remember much after that."

"When *did* you get into the pool?"

"Just a couple of minutes ago. I thought I'd go for a wake-up swim. You know. I was a little woozy." She started to giggle.

Christy failed to see what was so funny.

"Get a blanket, Antonia. Hurry."

Skeeter moved his hand away from the base of Mirinda's head and eased a cushion from one of the chaises under her neck.

"I don't think you should move, Mirinda. Let the paramedics tell us what to do."

"How did you learn to do mouth-to-mouth, Skeeter?" God only knew what else he had picked up. Maybe *he* could be senior beauty editor. Christy had taken a CPR class last year at *Allure* and had been terrified at the thought of mouth-to-mouth since then. Once, at *Le Bistro,* when a man had fallen over into his drink, a woman at a neighboring table had done it, pinching his nose shut and forcing panting breaths into his lungs. Christy had hung back, convinced she would have let the poor slob die.

Skeeter wrapped the blanket securely around Mirinda and held her hand.

What was Mirinda doing at the house when Tone wasn't there? Did she have a key? Quickly Christy dismissed the idea that she and Tone were having an affair. If they were, wouldn't he have been there with her, instead of off somewhere else, God-knows where?

Mirinda grabbed Christy's ankle.

"It's Tone's birthday, you know. Is that why you're all here?"

"Yes," said Skeeter. "We had a bad time getting out of New York. It's a mess. The snow, and all."

"I know. I told Tone all about it. But he wouldn't believe me. He had to do it *his* way."

That sounded familiar. He'd been doing it his way all his life. Suddenly Christy felt sorry for the poor wet Mirinda.

"What was his way?"

"He flew to Washington. Then, he was going to take some train to New York. He really wanted to see you guys. Said he couldn't stand the thought of not spending his birthday in the bosom of his family."

I'll bet, thought Christy. Bosom of his family wasn't exactly one of Tone's favorite expressions.

"Washington? When did he leave?"

"Yesterday sometime. I think it was morning. It may have been afternoon. What's today? What time is it?"

"Eight o'clock Saturday morning," Ed offered. Even the tug-o-wars with his mother and her lover hadn't prepared him for a conversation with the stoned Mirinda. Is that what Skeeter and I are like, he wondered? At least they'd had the self-restraint not to pass out. No one had ever had to call an ambulance for either of them. But of course there was always a first time.

The ambulance purred into the driveway and three tanned young men came toward them. After some preliminaries, they hoisted Mirinda onto a stretcher and moved her toward the ambulance.

Skeeter looked concerned. And smitten.

"Uh, Christy, I think I'll go with Mirinda. Just to make sure she's OK."

Tone's "freedom phone"—with antenna and push-

141

buttons—beeped over by the diving board and Antonia ran to answer it.

"Mrs. Lamb, Mother. For you."

"Oh, Lord," groaned Christy. She hadn't even had time to shower much less go to the bathroom. What in hell could Juneau want? Nothing good, that was certain. She was probably going to be chewed out for hiring Flemming Lord without Juneau or Reed's approval. Well, screw *them*. She was exhausted and she didn't feel like being charming. She didn't even feel like being civil.

"Juneau, darling, how are you?"

"Awful. Dreadful. I think I'm going to die."

"What's wrong?"

"I have the flu. This hideous blizzard. How in hell did you ever manage to get to the Coast?"

"Train to D.C., plane to L.A."

"Oh, Christy, love, you're so clever. I hate to call you out there, dear, but this is an emergency."

It all came back to her. The shoot. The trip to Nevis. The new photographer, Elizabeth. And Juneau was ill. Much too ill, it seemed, to go on a trip, even to a sunny, warm Caribbean island.

"Are you trying to tell me that you can't make the shoot?"

"Oh, Christy, love, could you help me out of this? Just one last time?" She wasn't going to tell Christy about the pregnancy. Not yet. She liked to keep her bombshells under control.

Christy stared into the pool's blue water. What choice did she have? If she refused, she'd probably be fired and what fun Tone would have with that.

"Of course I'll go, Juneau."

When she was a child, Christy had fantasized that one day she wouldn't have to study for exams or go to school on time or worry about pleasing her teachers or Aunt Vi and Uncle Harold.

Now was supposedly One Day. But Reed and Juneau had replaced her teachers; *Allure* had replaced school; and her articles, projects, and shoots had taken over for the exams. Would it ever end? Did Antonia and Skeeter have any such unreal concepts about the real world?

"Christy? Christy? Are you still there?"

"Yes, Juneau. I'm ready. They're setting up tomorrow. Shooting actually starts Monday."

"OK, darling. I sent the models down Thursday, before the airports closed. I thought they could all use a few days in the sun. That way, you won't have to use so much bronzer."

"Great. Is there anything I need to know? Does Elizabeth have any special quirks?"

Photographers were notoriously temperamental. Prima donnas. And Elizabeth was new. An unknown quantity. Christy wished they had gone with Alphone or Morgan Barbie. Someone she was used to working with. Oh, well, what could go wrong?

"Nothing that *I* know of, darling girl."

"Good. Oh, Juneau—since we missed each other Thursday, I don't know if you know or not, but I did hire that new assistant."

"Flemming Lord?"

"Yes." How the hell did she know?

"I'm ashamed to admit it, darling, but I adore his books. Have you read any?"

"Well, no. But I will." If she had to.

"I'd suggest you read one on your flight but Flemming is going to be with you."

Going to be with her? He was her new assistant... but a location shoot? As his first assignment?

"Flemming? Going with me?"

"Oui, oui, darling. You'll find a way to connect in Miami. I think you're both on Air Jamaica. Better check. You go to Antigua on a small plane. On second thought, dearie, you could read one of his novels on your way to Miami."

Christ. She had to wrap the Age Before Beauty article and clean up a few more important details, and now she was supposed to whip through a novel.

Maybe for once she should let Juneau have it. On second thought, maybe not. She'd just finished a 12-hour trip that would fell an astronaut. She was rumpled and distinctly untropical. She looked as though *she* needed a beauty editor. And anyway, she didn't want to say anything she'd regret later on. Juneau had total recall when it came to things like that.

"Maybe I'll take Antonia. She's never been to the Caribbean."

"No. You're booked into my room at The Golden Rock and there isn't any extra space for Antonia."

What was this all about? Juneau always had the largest room with a king-size bed so that Reed would be comfortable. It was almost as if she was throwing her and Flemming Lord together. "Well, Antonia will be disappointed."

"Darling, you can take Antonia to England in the spring. That'll make up for any disappointment, don't you think?"

"I guess. I'd better see about getting my body on a plane to Miami. I'll call you once we get to Nevis."

"Don't, Christy. It'll take most of the day. It's worse than calling from Rome. Just get the shots, lovey. Sensational ones. We're all depending on you. When you get back, I may have some sensational news. Bye-bye."

There was an 8:15 Eastern flight that arrived in Miami at 4 P.M. Forget that. A 9:15 Pan Am that arrived at 5:02. A TWA that left at 12:30, landing at 8:18. The 9:15 was safer since she had no idea when or how she was supposed to connect with Flemming. Damn Juneau and her

144

"you're in charge, darling. Get some great shots." As though with a wave of her lily white hand Christy could be magically transported to any place on the globe.

She glanced at her watch. The 9:15 was definitely the flight. She dialed Pan Am and booked herself in non-smoking, first class—it *was* an *Allure* trip, in the middle of a weekend, and it *was* her husband's birthday, after all.

Quickly, she showered and shampooed. She slipped into a white safari suit, red espadrilles and a blue silk scarf. She didn't look like she'd just been through a blizzard, a harrowing near miss with a boa constrictor on the Metroliner and an interminable transcontinental flight. She did have dark circles under her giant eyes, but it wasn't worth the bother of putting on cover-up. No one would know she was a beauty editor. She slipped on a pair of large, gray Dior sunglasses.

Where in hell is Tone, she asked herself for the tenth time that morning. He'd flow to Washington and taken Amtrak to New York. But he wasn't at their apartment. She tried one last time. Twenty rings. She hung up. If he didn't call soon, they'd miss each other. She'd have to leave him a note, like a runaway wife. Where could he be in New York at five in the morning?

She started pulling things out of her closet. Bathing suits, which she'd probably never get to wear. Editors weren't supposed to enjoy themselves. A nightgown and a peignoir. She only wore nighties when she was away—what if the hotel caught on fire? She cringed at the thought of having to stagger outside in the dead of night in her "Virginia is for Lovers" T-shirt. Sandals. Sun block. A bottle of cognac, just in case. Toothpaste. She always forgot toothpaste.

"Mother, why are you packing?"

An accusation.

"I have to go on a trip, darling. For *Allure*."

"What about Daddy's birthday?"

"But Daddy's not here, Antonia." Christy's mind was on the goddamn trip. She hated to travel on a moment's notice. If she'd been a foreign correspondent, there wouldn't have been any foreign news.

"Mother, I want to talk to you."

Christy stopped her packing, bottle of shampoo in hand.

"OK. What's up?"

"Are you and Daddy getting a divorce?"

What a question.

"Not that I know of. Why?"

"Well, I discussed everything with Ed. He said before his parents got a divorce, they didn't see each other much."

"Mr. and Mrs. Kurtz were legally separated, Antonia. That's why. And then Mr. Kurtz died. Your father and I love each other." Did they?

"Aren't you and Daddy separated?"

"Why no, Antonia." Christy sat on the edge of the bed and drew Antonia into her arms. "Of course we're not."

"Then, how come we live in New York and Daddy lives in Beverly Hills? Nobody lives like that unless they're separated."

"It's because of our careers. I thought you understood all about that."

"I understand that you work at the magazine and Daddy writes songs out in the pool house." She wriggled free.

"That's right."

"Well, they have magazines in Los Angeles."

"Yes, they do, darling."

"I went through all the magazines we have and all the magazines in the school library. Why can't you work for

Architectural Digest or *Bon Appetit*? You could go right down to Wilshire Boulevard instead of to the airport all the time."

Christy had seen this building up in Antonia for some time. The resentment. She was always dashing off, leaving Antonia behind. She couldn't take her most places. But Antonia would have loved the islands. She'd love Bath. Damn Juneau again.

"Antonia, I'm going to take you and Skeeter *and* Daddy to England in June."

"You are? Why didn't you tell me before?"

"Because I—I didn't know before. It was just decided."

"That's great. I've never been there. But Mother you still haven't answered my question."

What question? Christy had to start paying more attention. But it was hard when she had a plane to catch.

"Why can't you work for a California magazine?"

"Well, I can't work for *Architectural Digest* because I'm not an architect or a designer and I can't work for *Bon Appetit* because I'm not a chef. I can't even cook very well, Antonia. You, of all people, should know that."

Antonia shook her head impatiently. "Mother, sometimes, you just don't make any sense. You're not a hairdresser either, but you work for *Allure*. You're a writer and writers can *write* anyplace. That's what my English teacher says."

Stupid meddlesome English teacher. If she didn't start stuffing things into her bag, she'd miss the 9:15.

"In a way, that's true, darling. But I can't write for *Allure* anyplace."

"You can so. Most of your stuff you do on the plane."

"I do plenty of stuff on the plane. And at home in the kitchen and in my room and at the office. You know that."

Antonia was growing up. Fast. Christy had been such

a baby at her age. She hadn't asked questions. She'd been afraid to ask.

Growing up in New York City speeded one into adulthood, there was no question about that. Already Antonia used Christy's lipsticks and that revolting April Whore nailpolish or whatever the hell it was on her toenails. She was crazy for all the trappings of glamour. How could she escape it?

But there was more to this than just the outer manifestations of Antonia's growing up. She was questioning her mother's right to a career. Not to work—most of Antonia's friends' mothers did *some*thing. Charity things. Part-time things. But most of them seemed to have no real dedication to anything beyond money and family.

Marcy Kurtz. The perfect example. She worried about getting older, losing her looks. She anguished over her checkbook, convinced herself that she was in the throes of her last affair, her ultimate love.

Antonia stood staring at Christy. Her eyes were sad but tearless, wise and penetrating.

"Skeeter and I wish you'd quit and live with Daddy."

"You've discussed it, then?"

"Not exactly."

Christy knew Skeeter didn't give a damn where she worked or what she did. He'd probably be relieved if he could go back to boarding school again but there wasn't a boarding school on the East Coast he could get into. She'd never even considered the West Coast, he seemed to hate it so.

How could she explain to Antonia how much her career meant to her? How could she make an eight-year-old, even a precocious one, see that *Allure* held her life together?

There was nothing in Antonia's life that vaguely resembled Christy's childhood.

Rural Massachusetts in the early fifties had been everything 72nd Street and Rodeo Drive were not. There had been comforts but no luxuries. Aunt Vi and Uncle Harold had doted on her, shown her as much affection as they were capable of, but it hadn't been enough. There was no praise. Only lessons. Aunt Vi had taught her to cook, iron and sew—"the womanly virtues." Antonia wouldn't have had a clue what she was talking about.

Aunt Vi had no urge to do anything except be Uncle Harold's wife and teach piano. It was only when she attacked the old Sohmer upright that sparks began to fly. Chopin, Liszt, and her favorite, Bach's "The Well-Tempered Clavier, Book II." "I studied at The Curtis Institute," she'd say, whether or not anyone asked. It was her one departure from self-effacement.

Vi had tried to understand Christy, but they were just too different. She didn't realize Christy's thoughts were flying far from Hingham, Massachusetts.

Christy longed to go to New York. To the theaters, to "21," and the Stork Club—which she'd learned about from watching *All About Eve*. She had no illusions about marriage after she was graduated from high school. She was going to be a star.

She read everything. *Vogue* and *Harper's Bazaar* were her bibles.

Christy snapped back to reality.

"Why don't you help me pack, Antonia?"

"OK." Expertly, Antonia began to fold and roll her things into the bag.

"Where did you learn to do this so well?"

"From an article in *Allure*, where else? I always pack this way. How did you think I always got so many things in such a small suitcase?"

Christy felt a pang of guilt. Of course she'd never noticed—she'd been too busy getting herself together.

"Well! I always assumed that my daughter was a genius. And so you are."

For the first time that morning, Antonia looked as though she might be having a good time.

"Better now?" Christy lifted her chin.

"Uh-huh. I guess you can work at *Manure*."

"Antonia, I thought you hated it when Skeeter said that?"

"I decided he might be right."

The bedroom extension buzzed and they both pounced on it. Antonia won.

"Happy birthday, Daddy," she trilled. Then her face fell. "It's for you, Mother. The magazine."

Whenever Antonia called it "the magazine," Christy knew it was something, someone Antonia didn't approve of.

"Hello?"

Flemming Lord. She was to meet him in Miami. He'd arrange the flight to Antigua and the small plane to take them across to Nevis.

"I'll be on the 9:15. It lands at 8:18 this evening." Christy used her most businesslike voice.

Antonia was sitting on the bed, gazing into the bag when she hung up.

"How about some breakfast Antonia? Beverly Hills Hotel?"

"Can Ed come?"

"Of course. Why don't you go find him while I finish getting ready?" Christy said it carefully, afraid of sounding like she was dismissing Antonia. With all of her sophistication, this was the most sensitive child she'd ever known. Ed and Skeeter had the sensitivity of a plastic Jesus.

150

FIFTEEN

Washington, D.C.

DAMN BETTE. She'd been a mess when they'd been married and she was still a mess. Why should anything change?

How dare she check into a hospital masquerading as Mrs. Shaw? It had scared the shit out of him. And getting his ass over to George Washington University Hospital had eaten up a lot of his time. What a goddamn stinking way to spend your fiftieth birthday. No matter what they said about New York and Los Angeles, Washington was the worst city in the country.

Impossible streets. Lousy drivers. A killer climate. Marble monoliths that looked like they'd been churned out by PWA prison architects.

He'd been pleasant with Bette. She *was* Skeeter's mother. The only real achievement of her life and she'd been drunk at his conception. Tone shuddered. Sex with Bette. Wonder what she did with that man who'd been sitting in her room? Harrington something. Stamped out by the same cooky cutter that had produced Marcy Kurtz's live-in help. Christ. Who needed it? Even Jake Witt was preferable.

What was wrong with these women, fooling around

with guys like that? Maybe they weren't fags but they sure as hell weren't men, either. Men didn't do the dishes unless there weren't any clean glasses.

Christy must be in Beverly Hills by now. It was almost noon, practically nine there.

He called from a phone booth in the lobby of the hospital. Six rings. "Antonia? Sweetheart, how're things on the Coast?"

"Daddy! Happy birthday! Where are you?"

"Where I wish I weren't. But I'll be out there just as soon as I can hop on a plane. Where's Mother? She *what*? That eats shorts, all right. No, darling. Listen, is Skeeter there? He's where? Oh, God. I can't turn my back— what? Asleep in the living room. You mean to say that your mother went to Florida and left a naked man in the living room?"

He sighed. This was a happy, married life? Nobody could make a sit-com out of it. Too bizarre. But there wasn't much he could do until he got back.

"Listen, sweetheart, don't do anything until I get there. Yes, you can go for a swim. But only if Skeeter's there. Oh. Ed's OK, then. Have some lunch. Oh. Well, have a diet soda. I'll be home soon."

He hung up. Soon. Five hours plus.

When he got his hands on Christy, he was going to lay down the law. They were going to live together, in one place. He didn't care where. On second thought, he did. He could write songs on the East Coast. He already had. Practiced law, too. Self-fulfillment. Life style. Bullshit. What they needed were some roots.

Sixteen

New York City

"Don't you just adore my little plan, Reed?" Juneau snuggled up to Reed on her maroon satin Art Deco sofa.

"I think you may be in over your beautiful head, darling. For once in your well-orchestrated life."

What she had concocted was insane—even dangerous if anyone else ever found out about it. But now that he knew about the baby Reed would condone almost anything she did. Including this flight of folly.

"You know, love, that what I've done is the best thing for *Allure*? As much as we love each other, as much as we love Christy, *Allure* comes first, doesn't it?"

"What if your best-laid plan goes awry, my love? What if the trusting, hard-working Christy and the handsomest man in America don't hit it off?"

"Oh, Reed, how can they miss? Nevis is one of the most romantic islands in the world."

"Manhattan is a pretty romantic island, too, you know."

"Silly, silly person," smiled Juneau. "Remember when we were in Nevis. The Eighteenth Century Spa Look?"

"Four years ago, was it?"

"Seven."

"See how time flies when you're having fun."

"Corny, darling. It was magical there. The plantations, the champagne and lobster picnic, the sunset over the bath house."

"I remember fucking on the beach and about a thousand kamikaze mosquitoes drilling into my bare ass."

"They'll fall in love, Reed." If she'd been younger, if things had been different, she could have fallen in love with Flemming Lord herself. Of course, he didn't have Tone's money or connections or Skeeter. But what he *did* have was the potential to keep Christy right where she belonged: at *Allure*.

The magazine had to be kept in good hands. Juneau hadn't told Reed yet, but after the baby, what would happen if she got bored? Christy would let her come back. Some powerful outsider might make trouble, even if she were Reed's wife.

Besides, it made all the sense in the world. There was no way Christy could be editor-in-chief and still make the weekly commute to Los Angeles, keep up with Antonia and Skeeter's impossible demands and juggle Tone and his idiosyncrasies.

Juneau had decided to stay on for another month or so before turning the reins over to Christy. First, they had to get over the hurdle of the bikini shots with the new photographer. And they had to set up the trip to Bath. After that was the gala holiday issue.

As for Bath: She'd discourage Christy's taking the children. And then it hit her. Skeeter's mother, Bette Farmington, lived in London. Maybe she could talk Christy into leaving the kids in London. Brilliant. Keep them away from Flemming Lord.

"Scotch, darling?" Reed disentangled himself from Juneau's green silk Mandarin pajamas.

"Love one. It's OK, isn't it? I probably should be drinking milk or Ovaltine."

154

"How about milk punch? I used to drink it all the time when I had my ulcer. Two ounces of Scotch, ice, fill with milk, top with cinnamon. You'll eat it up, Mother."

Mother. Shades of the old homestead, where her parents called each other Mama and Pops. She couldn't decide if it brought a lump to her throat or made her want to gag.

"OK, Pops."

As he made a great show of going to the kitchen for some milk, Juneau decided she'd let Reed pamper her. That's what he wanted to do. Why rock the boat?

"God you're lucky," she told herself, as Reed returned with the milk.

"What did you say?"

"I was thinking out loud. That's all, darling."

"About what?"

"About where we'd be right now if I weren't pregnant."

"In Nevis, of course. Getting our asses bitten." He laughed as he stirred the milk punch. "Try that, Mom."

She sipped it. Not too bad. A little like the Junket she used to eat as a child. It was soothing, at least.

"A toast to the lovebirds," she said with a wink.

"To us, Juneau."

She'd meant Christy and Flemming Lord.

———————

Over the phone, Juneau Lamb certainly hadn't sounded much like the legend of *Allure*, Flemming Lord thought as he stuffed underwear and bathing suits into a pair of loafers and dropped them into the bottom of his Vuitton hang-up.

She'd announced herself in a meltingly seductive voice and then proceeded to give him orders. She'd talked about Christy Shaw like a doting aunt extolling the virtues of her eligible, if unattractive, niece. Almost like she was trying to match them up. What in the name of God was going on?

SEVENTEEN

Somewhere over the Great Mid-Waste

THE PLANE leveled off at thirty-three thousand feet.

Christy gazed across the empty seat next to her, and on out the window to a clear blue sky. She took several deep breaths, willing her body to relax.

Worrying wouldn't make Antonia understand her need to be part of *Allure*. It wouldn't make Skeeter see her as a serious person. Maybe he thought the magazine was frivolous, but, goddamn it, *she* wasn't.

Poor Tone. What a way for him to spend his fiftieth birthday. But secretly, she was almost enjoying his frustrations. Traveling was no fun. At least not the kind of traveling she did. Planes overbooked. Connections in the hands of the gods. Food in the hands of sadists. The only excitement the threat of disaster. Yes, Tone was finding out, the hardest way of all, what she went through every weekend just to be with him. Christy stretched and smiled.

She really had nothing against Beverly Hills. Its main fault was that it was a small town. Not anonymous enough. And, of course, *Allure* wasn't there.

She ordered a Bloody Mary with two vodkas and opened her attaché. What should she do first? There was the Age Before Beauty article to finish; four days worth of ideas submitted by her staff that she had to go over. And there was always the crossword puzzle from Thursday's *Times*. She opted for her editors' submissions.

Once a week, there appeared on her desk dozens of ideas whose time had gone. She began to read. Instantly her mind began to wander. She took out a lined, spiral notebook and a pen and began writing.

"Sometime after noon, Saturday. Dearest Tone, I'm in my favorite place: a plane, on my way to beautiful downtown Miami. I really wanted to spend your birthday with you, but our lives seem to have turned into an obstacle course lately. I think the kids are fine. Florence Nightingale has settled in for the duration. Mirinda is out of the hospital. She's fine. I turned off the thermostat. The pool isn't safe at any heat. I love you. I miss you. Christy."

She reread it. It didn't sound like her. She crumpled it into a little ball, dumped everything back into the attaché, snapped the top closed and slid it under her seat.

She'd try to call Tone from Miami. They'd probably get into an inane discussion about the thermostat. How could she make him see just how dangerous that hot water was? Maybe Mirinda could convince him.

She'd finished her Bloody Mary. Maybe she'd have another.

The hostess handed her a menu and she put it down. Who could think of eating? She turned to the window...

The dream was always the same. She was a child again, riding Spirit across the autumn fields, her unruly curls blowing wild and free.

Aunt Vi and a tall, willowy woman, dressed in a dark

city suit and a pillbox hat, are watching. Suddenly, Spirit shies at a stone wall. He stumbles. Christy is catapulted sideways. The woman in the pillbox hat gasps, her hand at her chest. Christy is sitting on the ground, Spirit is—where is Spirit? He's lying over there, he's hurt. Aunt Vi and the woman come running over. "Thank goodness she's all right," the woman is saying, distractedly patting her head. "Don't you think this is a bit dangerous?" "Never mind," Aunt Vi is saying. "We're taking good care of the child. Christina come inside. Harold, get your gun. Looks like Spirit's got a broken leg..."

Spirit is dead. They said it was the kind thing to do.

He was the only one she could talk to. Tell secrets to. Aunt Vi and Uncle Harold wouldn't understand.

She has never had anything she could call her own. Vi and Harold aren't her parents. Their home isn't hers.

Her sense of loss is paralyzing. She wakes up chilled, shaking. Part of her is here. Another part is still back there. Child and adult. Two pieces with no way she can find to push them together.

———————

"Bloody Mary, ma'am?"

Christy jumped.

"Sorry to startle you. But we'll be serving in about half an hour. I thought you might want another drink."

"Well, thanks. I'll have some wine."

She always seemed to have that damned dream when she had too much to drink. Her eyes itched. Her head throbbed. She wished she had a dollar for every word she'd written against drinking on planes. It doubled one's hangovers and jet lag.

"Red, white or champagne?"

"Champagne, please." At this point what could possibly make her headache worse?

How many years had she been trying to figure out

that dream? Going over and over it repeating it so often that the lady with the pillbox hat had almost become a real person...

She sighed and opened her attaché. She couldn't face the editorial suggestions today. Maybe she'd just throw them all away? God knows they weren't worth anything.

When she'd finished tearing up the countless sheets of scribble and scrawl and tucking them into the air sickness bags, only her spiral notebook, two pens and the article remained. She felt great. Purged.

The food arrived. She didn't even remember ordering. Whatever it was—pale, rubbery, coated with a ribbon of shiny goo—the mere sight of it turned her stomach. She sent it back and went back to sleep.

When she woke up, they were announcing the approach to Miami. She must have been more exhausted than she'd thought.

———————

Friends and relatives clustered in the waiting room. Skin tanned to the shade of the finest Cordovan. Arms like pretzel sticks. Flat asses. Birds' legs. Christy scanned the crowd for Flemming Lord's blond head. Instead, she saw—good God, could it be? Yes!—Tone with his old, navy cashmere coat slung over his arm.

Dazed, Christy smiled and waved. She was glad to see him. But what in hell was he doing here?

"Tone. Happy birthday."

Even looking so wholesome, so un-lawyer-like, in his old, effete Eastern snob clothes, he could make a kiss just about the sexiest thing in the world.

He looked at her tenderly. "Welcome to the Coast, Chris. How about a drink?"

"I'd love one."

They walked arm in arm into the terminal.

"I left your present in our room, Tone. Shall I tell you what it is?"

"No, goddamn it, you know I like to be surprised."

"And by the way...did you know that I've been chasing you all over Hell's half acre?"

She could tell he was about to spring something on her. Was he going to try to make her go back to L.A. with him? Well, she couldn't. It was that simple. He'd just have to understand. But he'd always gotten his way. A half century of self-indulgence didn't prepare one for a major "no."

They moved into a little bar, sat at the only vacant table and ordered two Scotches.

Tone touched his glass to hers.

"Now, my darling Chris, why are you in Florida? Antonia gave me some garbled version of the past few days on the phone, so I said to myself, screw it, Tone, get your ass to the Miami airport. There was only one flight you could have been on and presto, there you were." He leaned over and kissed her again.

Tone made her feel so lucky. So protected. She would never have admitted it to anyone, but she liked it.

"Well, I'll try to pick up where Antonia left off. I was unpacking...got in around seven this morning...the phone rang. Guess who?"

"Reed Doran and Juneau Lamb. Shit, it almost rhymes."

"If you put a rhyme like that into one of your songs, you'd never sell it. But you're right, it was Juneau. Commanding me to go to a shoot. She said she was sick."

"With what?"

"She didn't volunteer any information. Isn't that what you always advise your clients?"

He laughed.

"Anyhow, *she* can't go on the shoot so I have to go.

It's an important story, and we're using a new photographer. Elizabeth. You know how temperamental photographers can be."

"Selfish pains in the ass. More than song writers, producers and lawyers, all rolled up into one."

Christy began to relax. Maybe Tone wasn't going to try to make her do anything after all.

"That's it. She stays; I go. It should take two or three days, depending on weather, location. All that stuff. The photographer and the models are down there right now, scouting locations."

"Down there?" Tone asked suspiciously. "Down where?"

"Why Nevis, of course."

"Nevis, of course? Nevis, that little island in the goddamn forsaken, inaccessible Leeward Islands?"

"Yes," Christy said in a small voice.

"Have you ever *been* to Nevis?"

"No."

"Well, for Chrisakes, Christy, you could have said no."

"I could have."

"Why not? I thought you were going to quit that stupid magazine? You talk about it often enough."

"I know, I know. I think about it, but I just can't, Tone. Don't you see?"

"Don't I see *what*? That my wife is a nervous wreck? That my wife is exhausted, has no time for me, the kids, only time for her stupid *Allure*? You know, Skeeter's right: *Manure* is a terrific name for that piece-of-shit magazine. I'm getting another drink. You?"

Christy nodded. It looked like she was going to need it.

Tone slammed the drinks down on the oak-grained plastic table. "I don't want you to go to Nevis. I think we should spend a couple of days together right here.

In sunny Florida. Let some other asshole cover the shoot."

"*Some other* asshole?"

"Well—you're acting like one."

Christy fought the urge to jump up and run out of the bar. How dare he? Did she put him down for those stupid songs? But he was tired. He'd calm down.

"Why don't you come to Nevis, darling? I hear it has wonderful beaches. That's why Juneau chose it."

"Then Juneau should be down there putting her behind in one of them, along with that publishing whiz, Reed Dork."

"Doran, Tone. *Doran.*"

"Whatever. Look, I'm sorry, Chris. It's just that . . . that it's my birthday and I've never had a worse one. When I saw you, so gorgeous, skipping off that plane, I thought it's all worth it. Christy and I can spend a few days here. Away from the kids, away from L.A., New York and those brainless wonders over there in the Centurion Building. Goddamn stupid magazine can't even rent space in a decent-sounding place. What's wrong with the Seagram Building? Or the Chrysler Building? Je-sus."

If this were unavoidable, Christy sure as hell didn't know how to avoid it.

"Tone, you're so bullheaded."

"You're pigheaded."

"Stubborn as a mule."

"Dumb as an ox."

Tears slid down her cheeks. Instantly, his hand was on hers.

"I didn't mean it. I just couldn't resist. You know how I always carry things too far. Forgive me."

She always forgave him. Why not? What would not forgiving him solve? Would it make either of them happier? Richer? Thinner? More articulate? Better parents? Sexier lovers? Would it change anything?

163

"Darling," she said evenly, "life does not run like a Swiss watch."

One more time, it seemed, she was trying to erode his power base. Why? He didn't understand it.

He knew she wished she'd known her real parents. But she'd never told him much about her childhood so he hadn't pressed. *His* parents were sure as hell no prize. Captain Boston law firm and Miss Puritan. He'd been amazed to discover, in the course of writing a paper in his undergraduate days at Harvard, that the Puritans were the first group to champion marrying for love. Obviously his mother had missed the point.

"Christy, I'd like to come with you but I just can't."

"Why."

"Because it's *your* shoot."

"I'd come to a recording of *your* song."

"Oh, yeah? When? I've only asked you a hundred times."

"You haven't recorded a hundred songs, Tone." Damn. That wasn't fair.

"Clever. Clever. I know what you think of my songs."

"I love your songs, darling."

"Oh, no you don't. You hate 'Beverly Hills Babe.'"

"I never said that."

"You never had to. I could tell by the look on your face." Tone's voice was rising.

Christy stiffened. Sometimes his anger scared her. She'd seen him whip himself into a frenzy over nothing—a traffic jam, an elevator that wasn't ready and waiting when he pushed the button six times, an olive in his martini instead of a twist. In another minute, he would start to rant.

"Tone, please. You can lie on the beach in Nevis just as well as here. It'll be quieter. The water's warmer." Shit, why had she said *that*?

"If I want warm water, all I have to do is to get into

my swimming pool. But someone won't let me keep my pool warm. When I get back to the Coast, there will probably be ice cubes in my swimming pool." He tossed off the rest of his Scotch. He wanted to hit her. He wanted to hug her. Most of all, he just wanted to have a good time on his birthday. Was that too much to ask?

"Tone, please. Lower your voice." The bartender was eyeing them nervously.

"Good. Let him look. Let him stare. He can go blind looking at us for all I care."

"It's your birthday..."

"You're goddamn right it's my birthday. Am I having a party? Presents? A cake? *Fun?*" He took out his handkerchief and blew his nose loudly.

"This is the last time I'm going to invite you to Nevis, darling. You'd have a great time. Really you would."

"A great time, she says. Watching you run around, talking to some dumbass photographer who's fucking every model on the set? Listening to you blithering and blathering over the bathing suits or bras or purple lipstick or whatever this week's featured excitement is?"

"The photographer is a girl. She's new. Her name..."

"I don't want to hear her name. I want you to come with me to a hotel where I will call Ms. Juneau Lamb and do your resigning for you. That's what I want."

Christy stood up. Her drink sloshed all over the table. "It's too bad we can't always get what we want, Tone. I'll call you tomorrow. You know where I'll be if you want to reach me, or even if you change your mind and decide to join me. The Golden Rock, Nevis." She touched his shoulder briefly and walked out.

Christy walked blindly along, vaguely aware that someone was calling her name.

"Will Christy Shaw please come to the information

counter? Will passenger Christy Shaw please come to the information counter? Will passenger Christy Shaw please come to the information counter?" Finally, Christy started looking aimlessly for the information counter. Before she found it, Flemming Lord found her.

"Feel like another plane trip, Christy?" She looked dreadful. Her eyeshadow had smeared under her eyes. All her blush was gone. She wasn't wearing lipstick.

"Hi, Flemming," she said without enthusiasm. Be nice to him, her little voice said. After all, *he* didn't make you feel like shit. She smiled. "Do I have time to duck into a ladies' room before we board?"

"They're boarding right now," he said apologetically. "I think we'd better move it."

Christy groaned. There wasn't time to find Tone, to kiss him good-bye, to say something, anything, nice. She trotted along beside Flemming. He grabbed her hand, pulling her faster and faster until they got to the gate.

Every few yards, she turned back, looking for Tone.

———————

The last thing Tone saw was his wife and that blond nitwit, holding hands and smiling.

Eighteen

Nevis

FLEMMING WAVED his drink toward the window.

"When you see the central mountain on the island, you'll see why it's called Nevis."

"Oh?" The last thing Christy needed was a geography lesson. She was too busy hoping Tone was as miserable as she.

"You see, Christy, the island was discovered by Columbus in 1493. He named it *Nieves*—snow—because of the snowy clouds that hang above it."

Christy laughed for the first time since they'd boarded the plane. "I was hoping we didn't have to mention the word snow for the next few days."

"You'll like this little gem of an island, Christy. Historically, it's fascinating. Plundered by the Spanish, ruled by the French, then the British. The treaty of Versailles returned it to Great Britain. Know who was born here?"

"Nooo." Should she?

"Know who was married here?"

"No, again." At least Flemming was getting her mind off Tone and that depressing scene at the airport. Had Flemming witnessed any of it? Maybe he'd had her paged because he didn't want to go into that bar. Forget it— now she was being silly.

"Oh, Flemming. I feel like such a dope. Guess I've been involved with fine hair, oily complexions and split nails for too long."

She always felt insecure whenever anyone talked to her about something she'd never heard of. Aunt Vi and Uncle Harold had worked very hard to persuade her to go to college but she'd insisted on going to New York and taking her chances without "the advantages of a formal education."

"I've done a lot of research for my novels, Christy. My mind is a storehouse of facts. Anyhow, Alexander Hamilton was born here. Illegitimate. And Lord Nelson was married on Nevis to Frances Nisbit, widow."

"I didn't know Alexander Hamilton was illegitimate." Was she illegitimate, too?

"Indeed he was. His father deserted his mother to look for ways of making money. She died at thirty-two after going through every penny she had."

"God, it must be wonderful to know all those things, Flemming. No wonder you write so well."

"A-ha! You said you'd never read any of my novels. Now own up. Have you or haven't you?"

"No. But Juneau Lamb is a great fan of yours."

"Hmmm. Well, now that you know all about our island paradise, why don't you give me the drill about the shoot?" Flemming didn't want to talk about Juneau Lamb. He really didn't want to discuss the shoot either, but at least it was safer.

All he really wanted to do was touch Christy. Did she feel the same way? She was obviously tense. What had happened in California? She intrigued him. Fascinated him. More than any woman he'd met in...years? His life? He wasn't sure yet. But she was definitely someone special. What luck that Juneau had ordered him to Nevis.

Christy nudged him.

168

"Some shoots are horrors and some are a lot of fun. Usually, the photographer is the most important person, so that makes for a pack of prima donnas. We're using a new one this time. Elizabeth. I've never met her. She's a Juneau find. Juneau says she's very hot, but a little strange."

"Strange?"

"Apparently, she likes to photograph dead things."

Now he'd heard everything. Dead people? Animals? Flowers? Why would Juneau want anything like that in *Allure*? "By the way, Christy, exactly what are we down here to shoot?"

"New sun products. Girls in bikinis. Great beaches. You know. Mouth-watering scenes."

"Affluent fantasy."

"Is there non-affluent fantasy?"

It took Christy about ten minutes to unpack, brush her teeth and change into a pink striped silk gauze dress, the coolest thing she'd brought.

Nevis was wickedly hot and she was already getting clammy. She looked around the room. It was typical Juneau. Huge four-poster, hung with flowered cotton curtains. Great swaggy draperies. Plants. Several comfortable chairs, a chaise, a skirted dressing table, three round straw rugs. She pictured Juneau plunking down her eight Vuitton suitcases and a hatbox full of falls. Thank God *she* wasn't here.

Christy took one last look into her closet before closing the door. There was something so sad about the way her dresses hung there alone. Suddenly, she missed Tone more than ever.

He could have come to Nevis. If it weren't for his stupid pride. His male chauvinist pigheadedness. Well, she wasn't going to bend like a straw in his wind.

She'd always known that she couldn't spend her life waiting for a man to come home and relive his day for her over a couple of martinis.

After Antonia was born, she'd stayed home for two months. It felt like her life was going nowhere.

Part of it was having no adults around...she couldn't wait for Antonia to start talking, which of course was idiotic. Someday, Antonia would talk. And say things that would irritate Christy, just the way Skeeter did.

One day, she'd picked up the phone and called *Allure*. She was desperate to go back to work. She needed her life back.

It wasn't that she was feeling sorry for herself, exactly. It was just that she wasn't having any fun.

As beautiful and adorable as Antonia was, there was a limit to the amount of time Christy could spend with her. Being senior beauty editor at *Allure* answered "Who *are* you?" loud and clear. Motherhood didn't. The disappointment was deep.

"Damnit, Tone." Christy couldn't sleep. She grabbed a handful of Kleenex and drifted out onto the screened veranda in front of her room.

Golden Rock was glorious. A romantic sugar mill built just after the turn of the nineteenth century, on the side of a steep green mountain.

Christy gazed down the little stone path leading to the main building that housed the living room and dining rooms. It was a set, a backdrop. It could have been dreamed up by Juneau and six art directors. Frangipani trees, lillies, Royal Palms, Banyans, figs.

Flemming Lord was certainly a good explainer. He made her want to learn everything there was to learn about this little island.

She sank into one of the rattan chairs and stared at

the moon. Huge, white, full. It added to her restlessness.

What was the point of her life, *their* lives? The inane luxury of two expensive residences? The empty privileges of a two-career marriage? Had any of it made either of them happier?

She sure as hell wouldn't get much sympathy from Marcy Kurtz. And Aunt Vi wouldn't have been exactly thrilled with the mess she'd made of Tone's birthday. No cake, no present, no wife. Just a quick couple of drinks followed by a nasty, painful scene, with the wife and another man flying off into the sunset.

Jesus, they were a pair of strong-willed people. Much too strong-willed for their own good. Where was it going to end?

Christy went back inside. She might as well get into bed. She was too young for insomnia. Every year, *Allure* had at least one article about it. It was just anxiety and if she could get rid of her anxiety...she sighed as she slipped into a nightgown.

If Juneau were here and unable to sleep, she'd haul everyone out of bed for a production meeting. *Anything* to fill up the empty hours until the sun rose.

She glanced around the room. Where the hell was the phone? Forget it. Even if she were able to get through to Tone, she had no idea what she'd say to him.

She closed her eyes. Dear God, please don't let me have that horrible dream again. She put her arms over her head and stretched.

The last thing she heard was the lonely crow of a rooster.

———————————

"I don't believe it. I just don't believe it. It's unreal, for Chrissakes," the photographer, Elizabeth, mumbled between sips of iced Tang. "How in the name of all that's

171

unholy am I supposed to photgraph *them*? I couldn't even photograph them in black and white. And ladies and gentleman, black and white is not the name of the game. Not here in tropical splendor land."

Elizabeth was right. The three models sitting at the table were redder than a Mexican sunset. They were also covered with insect bites and blisters. One of them had green hair from swimming in the pool. They all had fevers, runny noses and bloodshot eyes.

Christy shook her head, nibbling at a slice of rye toast. "Got any brilliant ideas?"

"Yeah. When's the next flight out of here?"

Productive. Christy loved her attitude. Now she knew why Juneau hadn't bothered to come down. She wasn't sick at all. She was smart.

Flemming cleared his throat. "Excuse me, ladies. We need a model, right? Any beautiful girl who looks good in those bikinis?"

"Give that man the Albert Einstein award," Elizabeth said under her breath. "Yes, Flemming, that's exactly what we need."

"Then I propose we use Christy."

Christy gaped. *Her*? Plastered all over *Allure* in that leopard suit held up by God-knows-what?

"Oh, I don't think..."

"Done." Elizabeth jumped up from the table. "Get into one of those suits and we'll do a few Polaroid shots first, just to see. But I think you'll do. What's your name, anyway? I know you're not Juneau Lamb, the old cunt."

"Christy Shaw." What would Juneau have done? Ridiculous. Juneau couldn't possibly wriggle into a bikini. But at least this would save days of trying to find models and fly them down. "Give me about ten minutes. I'll have to put on a little bronzer."

"And a lot of sunscreen," Elizabeth added, pointing

172

imperiously at one of the poor things sitting across from them, "we don't want you getting a tan like *that*."

————————————

Elizabeth photographed Christy leaning against a Royal Palm near the crumbling Hamilton House gates, and later, on the majestic staircase of the ruined mansion. Over the years, the house had almost disappeared, surrendering itself to the voracious dark green undergrowth.

They dragged her to every beach on the island and finished, as the sun began to disappear into the dark water, at the Bath House, a cut stone Georgian shell where the rich and famous had congregated from as far away as the Court of St. James, more than two hundred years before.

Throughout the crowded day, Flemming Lord had watched intently, quietly offering suggestions to Elizabeth—who, contrary to her reputation, actually seemed to be listening. Christy had barely spoken to either of them. She was the center of attention, but she was totally alone with her thoughts.

She and Flemming were both eager to see the results of the sessions, but she knew they couldn't until they were all back in New York. Another two or three days wait after that, and Elizabeth would appear with prints. And then the fighting would begin.

Elizabeth would have her favorites. Juneau would have hers. Christy, hers. And Flemming would get into the act because he had made so many suggestions. It was the one aspect of a shoot that Christy hated. It just wasn't in her nature to enjoy harangues.

When they got back to Golden Rock, there was a telegram from Juneau.

"Darlings, hope you all don't have sunstroke by now

but Reed and I have discussed the photographs and feel that you must show maximum water stuff. Got that, kids? Nothing too arty; we're talking about sunblock for the beach. Let's keep it basic. Love and kisses, J."

"That's a piece of shit," Elizabeth said, sipping a rum and tonic. "We've got some great stuff. And water isn't a major part of it."

Christy frowned. Juneau was right.

"More tomorrow, Christy. Think you can stand it?"

"I can stand it. Maybe we should charter a boat. Nothing too grand. Just something that would give the impression of water. What do you think?"

"I'm not paid to think, Christy. At least, not by *Manure*."

Flemming swirled his ice cubes in his glass.

"Have you always called it that, Elizabeth?"

"Since I learned to read."

Which was yesterday, he thought, gazing at Christy. God, how beautiful she was, her face calm, serene, no sign of the irritation she had to be feeling thanks to this idiot. How could she put up with it year after year?

He was beginning to feel as though he'd last on *Allure* about as long it took to get back to New York—which, at the rate that things weren't going, could be a while.

Christy had changed. At first she'd seemed so self-confident. Now she seemed lost, uncertain.

How could all these supposed grown-ups take this shoot so Goddamned seriously anyway? What did it matter in the grand scheme of things if an ass puckered here or a thigh rippled there?

It was criminal that a lovely bright woman like Christy could be made to cower in the face of this teenage bully-ette. He wanted to take Christy into his arms, to protect her from this—this person. What or where was her last name anyway?

"I think the boat is a terrific idea," Flemming said slowly.

He could feel Christy's relief. She smiled weakly at him, then at Elizabeth. "I think Juneau will love that. She loves yachts."

"I'll go charter one." Elizabeth watched Flemming walk toward the main part of the old sugar mill.

"He moves well. Not at all the way I'd expect, but I haven't had time to observe him today. Too busy. How are you, Christy? Up to more of the same tomorrow?"

"Sure." She tried to sound nonchalant. She *was* beat, and she wasn't at all sure if she'd be up to it tomorrow. Even with the sunblock, the hat, scarves and cover-ups, her skin was dry, her hair salty and poison ivy or oak or something speckled the back of her thighs.

"I think I'll go shower, Elizabeth. It'll probably be some time before we get a boat."

"Here comes Mr. Masterful now. Better hang in for a sec."

Flemming was coming toward them.

"We can see four boats in the morning."

Elizabeth snorted.

"Yeah. And if we're lucky, one of them might be usable. Nothing is ever that easy, friends."

Unfortunately, Elizabeth was right. When they'd done the fragrance shots in Grasse, it had taken three weeks just to find the right garden and house and another week to find the right interior locations.

Flemming ignored her.

"Ladies, I think it's time for drinks and dinner. How about in the bar in fifteen minutes?"

———————

The bar was tiny, mahogany, and stocked with everything anyone could possibly think of. Elizabeth ordered

Scotch on the rocks. Christy and Flemming ordered rum and tonics.

Christy watched the bartender. "Flemming, what's he doing?" He had drawn four straight lines in a row on the bill, and when Elizabeth ordered a second Scotch, he drew a slanting line through the row.

"That's how they used to do it in English pubs. He might not know Arabic numbers."

What were *they*? Was there *anything* Flemming didn't know?

Dinner was announced and everyone in the bar moved into the low-ceilinged, stone-walled dining room. There were two oval tables covered in white damask, set with antique china and crystal.

Elizabeth poked Christy.

"I wonder if they're going to say grace?"

Christy was glad she and Flemming were sitting far away from Elizabeth. She found herself wanting to be alone with him. It reminded her of that night so long ago, when she'd first met Tone at Juneau's party. The night they'd spoken only to each other...

Now was a fine time to think of *that*. Concentrate on the food. Christy watched as an ancient black man in a white uniform so starched that it creaked ladled soup into the waiting porcelain bowls. "What's that?"

"Lobster soup. I think."

The man across from Christy leaned forward.

"It's conch chowder. An island delicacy."

It was strangely fishy, with ground rubbery pieces of conch, carrots, peas, onions and plenty of coarse black pepper. Christy finished it before anyone else. Instantly Aunt Vi was at her elbow. "Don't wolf your food, Christy. You weren't brought up in a barn."

Cautiously, she glanced around the table. No one was even looking in her direction.

After turtle steak, salad with chutney dressing, a huge basket of hottens—curried hot cheese biscuits—and some bananas au rhum, Christy began to worry. All that food and rum bulging out of a bikini? Maybe she should make an unobtrusive exit to the ladies' room and throw up. It was only a matter of seconds before Flemming would suggest a brandy with their coffee. Well, what the hell. Tomorrow she'd just hold it all in.

As they sat on one of the deliciously comfortable sofas, sipping demi-tasse, the models appeared, looking more bedraggled than ever. Christy's heart went out to them. They'd screwed up with *Allure*, which meant they'd probably lost several more jobs. Their hair needed several avocado treatments. And God only knew what their psyches needed.

"Maybe we should buy them a drink, Flemming."

"Glad to—" God, he almost said darling. What was wrong with him? "But I don't want to discuss the weather with them."

After coffee and brandy, Christy began to feel like she was caving in.

"Flemming, I'm about to do a Cinderella on you. I'm so tired, I don't think I could even..." her voice ran out.

"Even kiss me good-night?" He was immediately sorry he'd said it. "What you have, dear lady, is jet lag."

"I couldn't possibly. My body never had time to switch over to Pacific...from Atlantic, that is. Well, I guess this is good-night. What time shall we get knocked up, as they say?"

"Eight? Nine? The boat guys said any time before noon."

"Maybe we should make it early. If any of the boats looks right, we can start right away, and if not, we'll have more time to look for others."

177

"You win. But I insist on walking you back to your room."

"No, no, that's okay. Really. Anyway, the maid told me there's no crime on the island."

"How about tripping over a vine in the dark? Things like that?" He stood up, holding out his hand, and in a minute they were clambering up the steep little path, under a thick arbor, up some steps, past the pool, and into the moonlight.

Christy's heart was pounding. She wanted him. How corny and impractical could you get? She had Tone, Antonia, Skeeter, Juneau, Reed, *Allure*. Who needed more complications? Grief? Stress? She needed less. She needed a month at one of the spas *Allure* was eternally promoting.

He touched her arm. She jumped. If he touched her again, she didn't know what she would do.

She was lonely for Tone. She was lonely for *someone*. She longed to be held. She wanted Tone but Tone wasn't here because he'd said no to her invitation. It was all his fault.

Flemming's lips brushed hers again and again. She didn't pull away, she didn't kiss him back. She just clung to him, pulling him closer and closer until he began to push back.

"I'm sorry, Flemming," she whispered. "All those workouts at the gym. I guess I didn't know my own strength."

Flemming scooped her into his arms and carried her up the steps, across the screened porch and into her room.

"You didn't lock your door, Christy."

"No crime, remember?"

He turned the key firmly in the lock.

Instantly, she was back in his arms, her face buried

178

in his chest. He smelled like sun and the sea. She began to relax. They were alone. And they had time.

There was no privacy at 72nd Street, even less on Rodeo. Phones were always ringing, TVs blaring, feet pounding in the halls. Even locked doors didn't help. There were times when she'd been embarrassed to make love in her own homes.

Flemming had turned off all the lights. Moonlight poured in through the windows.

He was naked, his body outlined in the moon-flooded night.

He seemed vulnerable. More than Tone because he didn't hide it. He was spontaneous, inquisitive, open.

Tone had overpowered her. Flemming sparked her imagination.

He began to touch her breasts, moved quickly to her inner thighs, down under the backs of her knees and followed with his tongue. Feather-light flicks, until she was covered with goose bumps.

When Tone touched her, he touched every part of her the same way, with the same pressure. She'd never been able to tell him that different places needed different touches.

She realized, almost immediately, that she'd never have to tell Flemming anything.

Flemming leapt from the bed into the bathroom and returned with one of her sable brushes...for loose powder...and started tickling the soles of her feet.

Christy had been ticklish all of her life. She wasn't ticklish now. She squirmed with delight. Flemming moved to her underarms and nibbled at them before moving to her breasts.

He kissed them, long and lovingly for what seemed hours before moving down her stomach.

"Flemming, stop."

"No," he said gently. "I can't. You can't."

She didn't really want him to stop; it was just that she felt she'd scream or explode or lose her mind if he didn't.

Flemming began kissing her thighs. She quivered. "Flemming..."

"Hush."

He began biting her; light, tiny nips. She dug her nails into his shoulders and squeezed her legs together, willing herself not to come. Not yet.

Something slid under the door.

Christy froze.

"Relax, relax." He wrapped her in his arms. "What's the matter?"

"There's something under the door."

"No crime in Nevis, remember? It can't be a letter bomb."

"Let's see what it is."

"It'll keep."

"What if it's from Juneau?"

"It'll still keep."

Juneau. Flemming relaxed his hold on Christy, slowly rolled off the high four-poster and padded across the straw rugs to the door.

"Telegram."

"Open it, please."

"It's not addressed to me." He handed it to Christy.

It was from Tone. In L.A.

Elizabeth peeked into the dark windows of Flemming Lord's tower room. Nothing. She pushed at the heavy oak door. It swung open. No one.

Damn. Rats. She'd been convinced that he'd been coming on to her on the beach. All those suggestions. All that togetherness, peering into the camera.

He didn't give a shit about her; he'd actually been

180

trying to help make Christy look better. Not that she needed it.

Elizabeth sulked back to her room. Tonight wasn't going to be the only moonlit night in the luscious Leeward Islands.

Nineteen

Beverly Hills

WHAT DID Christy think their marriage was all about, anyway? Lately, she seemed to be playing it like one of those old Tracy-Hepburn comedies. Well, he was not amused.

He'd had more than enough time on the plane to go over it all. Why had he wanted to marry Christy in the first place?

Well, they'd fallen in love. And he'd loved the way she looked. He wanted other men to envy him when they saw her. He'd been impressed with her self-confidence, her ability to handle things. She'd been practically a kid and he *was* knocked out by the way she'd dealt with her career. She was still serious about it. Just as serious as he. All that had been great then but it wasn't now. All the things he'd admired about Christy were the factors that were fucking up his marriage. That simple.

No, it wasn't that simple. Nothing was. Money was a problem, too.

If he were poor, they couldn't have two homes. They couldn't afford the plane fares, maids, the Rolls, the pool, The Tutoring School, camp.

That was it. He'd sell the apartment. Then she'd have to move to Beverly Hills.

Tone smiled for the first time in days.

She'd be pissed. (He'd be extremely pissed if she tried to pull that on him.) But so what? It wouldn't be the first time. She'd get over it.

Jesus, it would be fun to have all of them in one place. No more of this gypsy caravan shit.

Why didn't she like L.A.? It was sunny, beautiful; the skies were blue most of the time. No blizzards. Most people would *kill* to live on Rodeo Drive. Why couldn't his wife be one of them?

"Hey, Antonia, Skeeter," he called from the kitchen door, "are you out there?"

No answer. "Antonia? Ed?"

He walked through the house. They had to be someplace. Everybody had to be someplace.

Where was Christy? He'd tried to get through on the telephone. He might as well have been trying to call a war zone in Central America. He'd sent a telegram. It would probably get there in two weeks.

Down there in that Godforsaken hole with the blond...blond...stallion. Well, if she wanted to sleep with him, it was her business. Damnit, it was *his* business.

Why couldn't she at least call him? Maybe she'd tried. She hadn't exactly been in a terrific mood when she'd stomped out of the bar in Miami.

Was she happy to go away with Lord or was it just that she was relieved to have left him behind?

You asshole, Christy asked you to come to that island. She begged you. He could kick himself.

"Kids? Where the fuck are you kids?" He was shouting now. He had a very low level of tolerance for frustration.

Tone crashed into the library. Ed, Skeeter and Antonia were watching a tape of *The Mummy* with the sound

184

turned off and *Aida* blaring from the stereo. No wonder they couldn't hear him.

"What are you kids doing?"

Antonia jumped up.

"It's fun. We all know the dialog from *The Mummy*. We've listened to it twelve million times. So...what goes with *The Mummy*? *Aida*. What do *you* do when you're bored with a movie, a TV show?"

"I don't know. Turn it off, I guess."

"Wrong, Daddy. You make it fun. No matter what you're watching, no matter how grundy, how boring, how utterly vomitous it is, the opera can save it."

"Save it?"

"Suppose you're watching an old Elvis Presley beach-type movie."

"OK." Tone had never watched an Elvis movie in his life.

"We know they stink."

"OK."

"So...turn off the sound and put on...say *The Marriage of Figaro*. You've got to have an opera, or some other weird vocal, because of the lip sync."

Lip sync? Was *he* losing his mind? Italian singing syncing with Elvis. He went to the bar and made himself a killer Scotch and soda.

Antonia followed him into the bar. "Daddy, you don't understand anything."

"Maybe you're right." He cradled her head against his chest, kissed her hair. She smelled just like Christy. "I love the idea of wiping out silly old bad-movie dialog with the opera."

"The news, Daddy. The news is the best."

"Whatever."

"Especially disasters. Fires and floods."

"Answer me something, Baby. Where do you want to

live?" He wasn't going to beat around the bush. Not any more.

"With you. And Skeeter and Ed."

Ed? Why Ed? "OK, tell me about it, sweetheart."

"I can't."

"Why not?"

"Well, I wrote to *Dear Abby*, and I'm waiting for her answer. As soon as she writes back or prints my letter in her column, I'll know what I should do."

Jesus. His own daughter couldn't even come to him or her mother with a problem.

"Why didn't you come to me? Or Mommy?"

"I didn't want to bother you. You're both so busy all the time. Mom's always going some place. You've got your clients and shows and the class. I mean, you're a big executive, Daddy. Everybody knows *that.*"

Big executive. Big jackass was more like it.

"What exactly did you ask *Dear Abby,* Tonia?"

"I mainly told her how miserable I was because my parents are nuts but I loved you anyhow."

"Why do you think we're nuts?"

"Because you love Mom and she loves you and you can't live together for more than two days at a time. I think that's nuts. If I ever get married, which'll probably be never, *I'm* going to live with him."

"I thought I was going to live with Mom, when we got married," Tone said wistfully. "But then things started to happen. I got busier and she got busier."

"Why do you two have to be so busy all the time?"

"Because we do, that's all."

"Oh, Daddy, answer the question. Please."

"Well, we need money to buy things. You know that. And things cost a lot, that's all."

"We don't *have* to have two houses, do we? If we lived in one place, we wouldn't have to have two maids and two cars and all those airplane tickets and taxis, would we?"

"No, we wouldn't. Look, sweetheart, I've been thinking about all the things you just said and I agree with you. We should live in one place. Not to save money but because I miss you and Mom and Skeeter. How about it, Tonia, how would you like to live here?"

"Here? On Rodeo Drive?"

"Right. Here on Rodeo Drive. Every day. We could go to some interesting places for the weekend. I mean, you and Skeeter and Mom wouldn't have to stay here every second."

"And Ed? Can he live with us?"

"Ed has a home, Tonia. What about his mother? She'd miss him if he came to live with us."

"He practically lives with us now. He sleeps over almost every night. Anyway, I like Ed, Daddy. He's funny. I'm never sad when he's around."

Tone put his arms around her. "Antonia, I don't want you to be sad. Not ever. Not for a second."

"I can't help it. Don't you ever get sad, Daddy?"

Sad. Chasing Christy across the country and down to Miami, only to have her jump on a plane with a good-looking guy was enough to make anyone sad. And why? She said she loved *him*, no one else. Not ever.

Christy must have had plenty of opportunities to hop into the sack with someone. Someone younger, handsomer, sexier. But she hadn't. At least, she said she hadn't.

He couldn't dwell on that now or he'd really be sad. And that certainly wouldn't make her any less sad.

"Tonia, I think we should discuss where you'd like to live."

"You mean here or New York?"

"Right."

"I don't care. I just want us all to live together. And

I don't think Ed's mother would miss him. She's too busy with her boy friend."

"What about friends at school?"

"I don't care. I'll get some new friends. Besides, who needs friends when you have Skeeter and Ed?"

"OK. Then it's settled. We're all going to live here. I'm going to sell the apartment in New York."

"But what about Mom? What if she gets mad or something and says she wants to stay in New York?"

"I'll wait until she comes back from her trip. We'll sit down and work things out. Like we just did."

Antonia threw her arms around him. "Oh, Daddy, I hope you can pull this one off."

"My darling, Daddy intends to pull this one off."

"Dad," Skeeter said as he and Ed came out of the library, "you should have watched *The Mummy*. It was greatness itself. Anybody interested in getting some pizza?"

Antonia yawned.

"I don't know. Maybe you could bring us some back. I think I'd like to go swimming."

"Well, what kind do you want, your highness?"

"The same delicious kind that's all over Mom's white carpet, Skeets."

"That means anchovies, and sausage with extra red pepper."

"Get a really big one. Or, two. I'm going to be starved after I do some laps."

"Man oh man I think I died and went to heaven." Ed sat in the back of the Rolls Corniche convertible with Doctor Watson draped around his shoulders as Skeeter drove down Rodeo Drive toward Wilshire Boulevard.

"Tell me, Shaw," he continued, toying with Doctor Watson's tail end, "where is the chicest pizza parlor in Beverly Hills?"

"Spagos. You won't believe it. People in there with thirty-carat diamonds stuffing pizza into their exquisitely made-up faces."

"Men don't wear makeup."

"You better believe it. Hey, maybe you'd rather go to Mr. Chow and get some french-fried seaweed?"

"I don't think that stuff is seaweed. I think it's the clippings from all the lawns on Rodeo Drive."

Ed tumbled into the front seat with Skeeter. "Doctor Watson likes the sights, Skeets. Nobody looks at him out here, the way they do in New York."

"Out here, Ed, Doctor Watson is just another pretty face."

"Pizza ahead."

"Better get one for Watson, Skeets. I'll stay in the car with him. Once he gets a whiff of that hot, crusty, tomato-infused, oregano-slathered, sausage-impregnated deliciousness, there's no telling what he might do."

"Anchovy *garni,* right?"

"Is the Pope Polish?"

"Listen, I don't think we should eat any of this stuff in the car. If we get it on the hide upholstery, forget it."

"OK, then. Home, Shaw."

"Want to drive, Ed?"

"Can I? I've never driven a Rolls-Royce in my life. I've never even ridden in one until today."

"Live big." Ed slid behind the wheel and they purred down Wilshire Boulevard toward the Beverly Wilshire Hotel.

Unnoticed by Skeeter and Ed, Doctor Watson slith-

189

ered toward the boxes of pizza in the front seat. He
managed to wriggle under Ed's foot, around the gas
pedal, and up Ed's leg.

"Hey, Watson," Ed yelled, looking down at the snake.
"Skeets, get him off, will you?"

Skeeter did his best to dislodge Doctor Watson, but
it was too late. The Rolls careened into the entrance of
the Beverly Wilshire Hotel, lurching to a stop on one of
its large, ornamental wrought iron gates.

TWENTY

Nevis

IT WAS the morning after nothing happened.

Tone's telegram couldn't have arrived at a worse time. Or a better time, depending on your point of view. She'd spent a sleepless night thrashing around in bed. Flemming had spent the night in his mill tower.

Her longing for him had reached an unbearable intensity. Was it the same for him?

"Breakfast?" Flemming called from the screened porch.

They had to look at the boats. More photographs. Elizabeth. Christy ached everywhere. She stretched. How did models manage it? She could barely stand up.

"Coming."

What was she going to say to him? Sorry about last night? It was great fun while it lasted? At least he was still talking to her. Or so it seemed.

"Hi," she said shyly. Why the hell did her hair have to be wet?

"Room service."

He was wearing a white silk shirt and dark green shorts, and his skin was a burnished bronze. He hadn't burned at all. And he was even sexier (was it possible?) than he'd been last night.

"No bad news, I hope," he said coolly.

"No. Not at all. Just something domestic. You know."

Tone had apologized for being a horse's ass. He missed her. He wished she'd come home. He sent all his love.

Christy looked at Flemming. She loved him. It was that simple. No one had ever struck her so immediately, so overwhelmingly.

Sometimes, her editors at *Allure* had told her of their conquests; how they'd asked men to go to bed with them. Just like that. No romantic dinners. No seductions. No intrigue. Christy had been shocked. They'd been missing the best part. She loved romance. She adored "settings." And so had Tone. Master of the grand gesture. The magnum of Dom Perignon. The antique jewelry. The flower on her breakfast tray.

Flemming held a crystal goblet of orange liquid up to the light.

"How about a glass of Tang, Christy? They don't seem to have oranges on the island."

As Christy reached for the goblet he put it down and pulled her into his arms. She clung to him, feeling as though her heart would burst out of her body and through her thin, peach silk robe. Why had she worried about what to say? She didn't have to say anything.

They collapsed on the bed. Flemming tore off his shorts and entered her immediately. A few frenzied, desperate moments later, at once and at one, they were racked by a breathtaking climax. They lay drained, holding each other close.

"I'm sorry," he gasped. "I guess I've thought of nothing else for the past twelve hours or so."

"Don't move. Please." Christy drew him closer with her arms and legs.

192

He smiled.

"I don't think I can move. I certainly don't want to."

She was hot and cold; happy and miserable. Her face was wet with tears.

"What is it, Christy? Are you OK?"

"Nothing." She tried to hold back her sobs. She couldn't let this go any farther, but she felt powerless to stop it.

Making love had never been like this with Tone. If those steamy novelists knew what they were talking about, this was what sex was supposed to be like. How she'd prayed for this with Tone. She trusted him. She loved him for his faults. And yet she'd not only let this happen now, with Flemming, she'd actually encouraged it. Welcomed it.

"Christy," he asked gently, "are you sure you're OK?"

"Never more OK."

"Did things...well...happen with you?"

"Things happened."

She'd never wanted sex for its own sake. That was about as interesting as a workout at the gym.

She wanted someone who wasn't too busy, always running off, constantly on the telephone. Someone, quite simply, who cared. About *her*.

When Christy and Flemming arrived at the dock, Elizabeth was hard at work taking pictures of dead fish.

Flemming grimaced.

"Hope she doesn't have any ideas of using that background for the *Allure* shots."

"It's her quirk. You know how she started in photography, don't you?"

"Do I?"

"Weren't you the one who told me? She and her younger sister were riding their bicycles on 72nd Street and a bus got her sister. There was nothing anyone could do except wait for an ambulance. She started snapping like mad. Eventually, she became a photographer."

"That's about the wildest thing I've ever heard."

"What do you think of these boats?" Elizabeth pointed at some fishing boats and a row boat.

Christy looked.

"Well, I suppose we could get some rustic shots on them...but I don't think that's exactly what Juneau has in mind. I think we need a luxury yacht."

"Agreed," snapped Elizabeth. "I radioed Grenada Yacht Service. They just happen to have a sixty-five-foot schooner for charter. Captain and one in crew. We fly to Grenada and we're all set."

"Where's Grenada?"

"In the Grenadines."

TWENTY-ONE

Beverly Hills

"HELLO, MOTHER?" Tone shouted into the phone. The connection crackled across to North Andover, Massachusetts. "This is Tone. Tone. Anthony Shaw. Your son, Mother."

"Why didn't you write, Tony darling? You're running up your phone bill."

"Someone was using my pencil," he mumbled. "This is an emergency, Mother."

"Who died?"

"No one died, Mother. Listen, I want to sell the apartment in New York. Do you have any objection to that?"

"Why should I? It isn't my apartment. If you can't make up your own mind about whether or not you should sell your own apartment, I don't see how I can help you. From what I've heard it wouldn't be such a bad idea—my friend Clara, you know Clara don't you? Well Clara told me everyone knows you're going to hell in a hand basket."

"It's not that, Mother. I just don't think I need two homes anymore."

"You never did, Anthony. Why don't you move to North Andover? The neighborhood has stayed the same for over two hundred years. No undesirables up here, you can be sure of that."

God, undesirables. The battle cry of his youth. Undesirables invaded neighborhoods and ran down the property values. All the places they'd ever lived, with the exception of North Andover, had suffered the same fate.

"That's a nice idea, Mother, but I'm not sure if Antonia and Skeeter would like living there. They're used to a more urban environment." Careful, Tone, you're skating on thin ice or walking on eggs or something.

"Urban environments are awful for children. You should know *that*, Tony, dear. Didn't you learn anything at Harvard?"

The most important thing he'd ever learned was when to keep his mouth shut, and he hadn't learned it at Harvard.

"Yes, Mother. Listen, how are you? I haven't seen you in some time. How long has it been?" That was innocuous enough.

"Almost two years, Tony. You're a disgrace to the Shaws. Likewise, the Grantlands. Your grandmother Grantland would tan your hide if she were alive today."

"Yes, Mother. Now, about the apartment..."

"Anthony, let me make myself clear. I haven't set foot in that apartment since V–Day. What on earth makes you think I care one whit if you unload it? At the rate real estate seems to be going in New York, you could make a nice profit on the dump."

"That's what I'm getting at, Mother. I think I owe you some of that profit."

"You don't owe me anything, Anthony. I just want you to be happy and stay away from drugs. You young people frighten me."

"Mother, I'm fifty years old. The strongest drug I take is an occasional aspirin." Like now.

"Well, darling, it's been awfully nice speaking with you. Let me know what happens with that apartment."

"Right, Mother."

"And darling, have you noticed if that Japanese bronze is still in the living room? It's an urn."

Japanese bronze? Japanese bronze? Japan—oh, Christ. "Does it have dragons, sort of carved, on it? Six-sided?"

"That's the one."

"I took it to California, Mother. It's in my living room."

"That bronze is too good for California, Anthony."

"Right you are, Mother." Christy had had it made into a lamp.

"Take good care of the bronze and let me know...by letter...what's going on with the apartment."

"Yes."

"And dear, happy birthday. Did you get that red robe I sent you?"

"Oh, yes. As a matter of fact, I just dropped you a note about it. It's sensational." It was in one of those piles on his closet floor. He thought it had fallen off the back of a truck.

"Good, dear. Now get off the phone before you use up all that glorious profit you're going to reap from selling that revolting apartment."

"Bye-bye, Mother." But she'd already hung up.

That was Sarah-Jane Grantland Shaw. One short mention of the kids and then not by name. She never asked about Christy. She didn't seem to be able to tell Christy apart from Bette, so she forgot about them both. He yawned.

He was going to unload the apartment before Christy got back from Nevis. Was it possible? At least he could put the wheels in motion.

He'd just hung up on the third broker when the phone rang. Ed. He and Skeeter and Doctor Watson were at

the Beverly Wilshire Hotel, and could he come down
there right away? Nothing serious. Yet.

"Cheer up, Dad," Skeeter said bravely. "I tell the nurses
I'm in for a sex change operation."

"Yeah, Skeets. Too bad the old one-liners couldn't
keep you kids on the road."

Skeeter lay in bed at Cedars–Sinai Medical Center,
sipping apple juice through a bent straw. "I can get out
of here, Dad. Tomorrow morning, just as soon as they
X-ray my balls."

"Will you please quit the comedy routine and tell me
what the hell happened?"

"Dad, you know everything I know. What did the cops
say? Plenty, I'm sure."

"Reckless driving. You weren't drunk. No pot, no dope
of any kind. Smart, for once. The car wasn't stolen.
Basically, they just couldn't understand how in hell you
could drive out of your lane, across the street and into
the driveway of the hotel, right into their iron gate. I
must confess, Skeeter, I find it a little hard to understand
myself."

"It was really Doctor Watson's fault."

"Doctor Watson? You kids were driving around Beverly Hills in a convertible, with the top down, with a
Goddamn boa constrictor?"

"Well, yeah. Anyway, Doctor Watson loves pizza, right?
And so he was going nuts trying to get at it. He crawled
under Ed's foot and around his leg. He tried to move
him. The car got into the wrong lane. Ed swerved to
miss a Mercedes and pow, right into the gate. That's the
bottom line, Dad."

"The bottom line, Skeets, is three thou for the car
and almost twice that for the gate. Seems you dented

198

the stucco or the cement or something. Quite a trick. Goddamnit all, don't look so stricken. Most of it's covered."

"Shit, Dad, I guess I shouldn't have let Ed drive."

"Look at it this way. If you'd been driving, Ed would be lying here waiting for the X-rays and Mrs. Kurtz would be X-raying my bank account. Where *is* Ed, anyway?"

"He took Doctor Watson home. I didn't think either of 'em would be too happy here. Besides, after all that trauma, I thought they could use some pizza."

"Very thoughtful of you." Tone shook his head. What had he and Bette created? "Listen, Skeets, I want to have a serious talk with you."

"Dad, I've been to bed with several girls. I don't have herpes. I don't snort coke. And Harvard is never going to let me in the front door."

"Good. *Now,* I want to have a serious talk with you."

"Shoot."

"I'm thinking about unloading the apartment in New York. We could all live here on Rodeo Drive. What do you think?"

"What do *I* think or what do you want me to tell you?"

That remark caught Tone up short. Was he that much of a tyrant? He didn't think of himself as a tyrant at all. He was quite lovable. Charming. Talented. In a good humor. A good-humored Renaissance man.

He plunked down on the vinyl chair next to the bed. "Am I that much of a bastard?"

"You? A bastard? C'mon, Dad. You're not even in the ballpark with famous bastards. Mrs. Kurtz, for example. She gets four stars."

"Then why did you say that about telling me what I want to hear?"

"Because that's the only time you listen." He paused.

"Go on." Might as well get it all out in the open.

"You want your own way, right? And Mom wants her own way, right? Antonia and I are in the middle, with no rights. We've got sore necks from being jerked around by our choke collars. Know what I mean?"

"You mean, we never ask you what *you* want to do, right?"

"Sort of. But it's more than that...it's as if it doesn't matter what we want to do. I mean, suppose I have a date or something, I still have to get on the plane, if Mom says so, and come out here."

"Do you like it out here?" Please let him say yes.

"I didn't use to, Dad, but it's growing on me. I think watching Ed's reaction gave me a whole different picture, you know?"

"Ed's pretty knocked out, huh?"

"Yeah. And he's not exactly your basic hick."

"Think you could come out here to live? With me? Contrary to what Mom says, they do have schools out here. And by the way, that crack about Harvard a few minutes ago. I never said you had to go to Harvard...or any place else, for that matter. I just want you to learn something." Their eyes met and locked. It dawned on Tone that he hadn't told Skeets he loved him in—in months? Years? But that was what *he'd* grown up with.

Sarah-Jane Grantland Shaw had never, as far back as he could remember, ever kissed him. Somehow it didn't matter any more.

"Dad, I'd love to live with you," Skeeter's voice cracked. "We could have a ball, couldn't we?"

"*I* think so, Skeets."

"There's something I forgot to tell you. I didn't *exactly* forget, I just didn't."

"What's that?"

"I saw Mom at Dulles."

"Well, I *know* you saw Mom at Dulles. So did Antonia, so did Ed."

"No, Dad, I mean I saw *Bette*. She said she was coming to your birthday party. She was with some backgammon guy from London. He wasn't exactly captain soignée."

"Oh. Well, Skeets, I saw her, too. I told her I wasn't having a birthday party."

"Did she believe you? Maybe she'll show up."

"I hope she went back to London or back to somewhere else."

"What's wrong with her, Dad? I mean she is my real mother and everything."

"Do I look like Anna Freud? I spent years trying to figure out what was wrong with Bette, with me, and I never even got close to the problem."

"Give it a guess."

"She's a spoiled brat. If she can't have her own way, she makes life hell for everyone around her. I couldn't stand it any more. I know. I know—I have to have my own way, too. But what's *wrong* with that? I'll tell you. No give and take. That's what's wrong with us and Russia."

How the hell he had gotten from Bette to Christy to Russia was beyond Skeeter. Well, when in doubt, align yourself with a parent. "So, Dad, what's our next move?"

"I'm going to sell the apartment."

"Christy will probably divorce you."

The possibility had never even entered his mind. Divorce him? But she loved him, worshiped him.

"Don't be an ass, Skeeter."

"Dad, she loves that sleazy magazine. And Juneau and Reed. The whole bunch. She forgets what day it is when one of them gets on the horn. They own her."

"You're kidding."

"I'm trying to tell you. You just don't want to see it.

That frigging magazine is more important to Christy than all of us put together."

"Don't say that, Skeeter." Would she divorce him if he got rid of the apartment?

"Dad, maybe you aren't the world's greatest understander of women, but if you stayed with us in New York for a couple of weeks, you'd see what I mean. You only see Christy on weekends. I wouldn't push it, if I were you."

Where did Skeeter get his insight? Did he know what he was talking about?

If he sold the apartment, which he intended to do, and Christy asked for a divorce, he couldn't afford it. Not Christy and Bette, too. And Skeeter and Antonia.

Shit. He was in the top .03 percentile and he'd have to live like a pauper. He'd have to sell the Rolls. That really hit him where it hurt. He couldn't sell the Rolls.

"OK, big man, what do *you* think we should do?"

"Well—Dad, you're so wild. You get an idea and you tear off into outer space before you've thought it through. Just like you used to tell me I did when I was being a pain in the ass at Blair Academy."

Blair Academy. Tone had been trying to forget about that phase of Skeeter's life. The midnight phone calls. Telegrams. Letters. Threats. And the final blow, expelling Skeeter the day after they'd cashed Tone's check for second semester's tuition.

They'd been right. Skeeter was a hell-raiser. How had he gotten so wise all of a sudden?

"Skeets, my boy, there may be truth in what you say."

"Think about it Dad...at least overnight. I bet you've already been on the phone to some New York real estate brokers."

Jesus, did the kid have ESP? This was beginning to give Tone the creeps.

"Guilty."

"And, Dad, remember something: You love show biz, your songs, your acting class, producing TV shows, being a lawyer five minutes a day...see what I'm getting at?"

"Not exactly."

"Christy doesn't love all that stuff. When you live out here, Dad, you've *got* to be in TV or movies. I mean, for Crissakes, even your dentist talks about getting on Johnny Carson."

Tone put his head in his hands. Skeeter was right. Shit.

"Look, Skeets, they'll probably bring you a rubber chicken and some rice pudding for dinner. Let me get you some pizza or Chinese. A couple of beers. Huh?"

"That's OK, Dad. I hear the food here is great. But there is something I'd like. That is, if it's not too much trouble."

Nothing was too much trouble. Skeeter wasn't badly hurt. Ed wasn't hurt at all. Everything was fine. Except for that damn gate, some cement and the love of his life, his Rolls.

"Name it."

"Well, you mentioned Chinese...how about an order of fantastic lobster and some of that French-fried seaweed from Mr. Chow?"

"Skeets, I don't think Mr. Chow has take-out. Maybe for a yacht or a private jet—"

"Tell them your only son has twenty-four hours to live. He's lying in a coma at Cedars–Sinai and he can only say five words: Mr. Chow's French-fried seaweed."

Twenty-two

Grenada

Sleeping with Flemming had plunged Christy too quickly into something she definitely wasn't prepared to handle. He'd taken her breath away, in the old-fashioned, romantic sense, and she didn't even know him. But how *could* you know someone in just five days?

Lately, she'd been so lonely without Tone, so frustrated, so trapped at *Allure*. Maybe Flemming was just a way out.

She remembered how at first she'd thought Flemming was flattering her just to get hired. Maybe he *didn't* really love her. And even if he thought he did, how could he be sure? How could she? Christ. It was all so confusing.

When she'd first met Tone, she had been caught up in his wine-dine-sex-and-bullshit approach. She'd worshiped him.

She moved the ice bag lower on her forehead. The heat was overwhelming. The *Eau Cristal* seemed to be wallowing at anchor. She was the only person on the schooner whose hair wasn't in tangly strings.

The models were on deck, posing in hats and scarves, their splotched bodies slathered with bronzer and makeup. Elizabeth had promised just a few more shots and they could wrap for the day.

Christy reached for the glass of ice water beside her bunk. She felt like hell. Could guilt make you sick to your stomach? Maybe it was food poisoning. How the hell was she going to make it back up to the deck?

She closed her eyes and shifted the ice bag on her throbbing forehead. Maybe she should take her temperature.

She'd tried everything. Bufferin. Di-Gel. Dramamine. Alka-Seltzer. *Nothing* had helped. She rolled off the double bunk and lurched to the bathroom. She hadn't been this sick since she was pregnant with Antonia.

A shiny, red face stared back at her in the mirror above the tiny oval sink. Were those *her* yellow eyes? She couldn't let Flemming see her like this—and forget Elizabeth's cruel camera.

She turned on the tap. Warm water trickled onto her hands. She splashed her face. She took the ice cubes out of her ice bag and rubbed them along her forehead, around her cheeks, under her eyes. Almost immediately she felt better. She patted some ice on her wrists and ankles.

What she needed was a shower. But the boat's water supply was short. At least her cabin was pretty. Wall-to-wall carpet, *toile*-curtained portholes, walnut paneling.

She began to work on her face with bronzer and blush. In a few minutes, she looked as though she'd spent a month cruising the Caribbean in style.

She slipped on the pale yellow maillot and tied its strings into a bow at the back of her neck. The sexiest neck in the world, Flemming had called it last night.

Last night. Had she been too aggressive? *She* had seduced *him*. She'd never done that with Tone. It had never occurred to her that he might like it.

It occurred to her now that despite his Beverly Hills image, dazzling, inviting smile and suggestive nonsense,

Tone was actually a little stuffy. For years she'd suspected that if anyone ever took him up on his flirting, he'd run away. Fast.

Christy brushed her hair and scrunched her curls with her fingers. She was ready to go up on deck. But the thought of seeing Flemming...it had been several hours. He'd been taking his job very seriously, checking all the shots, making sure the bronzers and blushes were shown to advantage, trying to appease Elizabeth and still keep things moving along.

"Oh, Flemming," she said under her breath, "what am I going to do?"

As she climbed the short flight of steps to the deck, she was overcome with a wave of dizziness. Her legs turned into rubber, her hand let go of the brass handrail, and she fell backwards down the steps.

When she came to, she was lying in her queen-size bunk and Flemming was kissing her.

"God, I think I passed out."

"You did. The captain thinks it's the heat. Says it's very unusual for it to be so hot this time of year. Once we're under way, things will be a hell of a lot cooler."

"I hope so. I thought Tone's pool was the hottest place I'd ever been, until we got to...where the hell are we, anyway?"

"On our way to St. Vincent. Elizabeth stopped snapping the models and shot a few rolls of some natives killing a turtle."

"Ugh. Why did you have to tell me that?"

"It seems we're having the turtle for dinner."

Christy groaned.

"You like turtle soup, don't you?"

"I never thought there was turtle in it. Like Welsh Rabbit. There isn't any rabbit in *that.*"

"Adorable girl." Flemming gathered her in his arms.

What was this adorable stuff? She hated the word—too sticky. "What's Elizabeth doing now, Flemming?"

"Getting a few last shots. She wants to shoot a couple more of you with the sun going down."

"I don't know if I can."

"It's a lot cooler now and soon we'll be under way." Flemming got up, and cradling her like a child, carried her up the steps.

The sun was falling behind the three graceful masts of the staysail schooner, into the light green shallow sea on their port side.

Elizabeth turned toward them as they ascended.

"Oh, hello Christy, darling. I hear you're in heat." She snapped a few shots.

"You got it, Elizabeth," Christy said gaily. "Now, let's make this a wrap, shall we? Juneau's dying for these shots."

Elizabeth looked at her in amazement. Most people jumped at her baited remarks and made fools of themselves. It was almost as much fun as photographing dead anythings.

"OK, let's go. Christy, over by that table. Pick up the champagne. You're going to drink it. You're thinking about your lover. What a good fuck he gave you in the sack last night. Smile. More Mona Lisa. Enigmatic. Less teeth. OK. Good. Great, more profile."

Christy's mind began to wander. God, this was boring. Doing things on command. Dogs had more fun. But listening to Elizabeth was mildly entertaining. While all photographers kept up a running banter, hers was guaranteed to chafe. Juneau claimed that was how she got such interesting results.

After an hour, Elizabeth called it quits.

"That's it. No more film. Let's have that champagne for real."

They were under way. In an hour, in the last light, they'd arrive at St. Vincent, where Elizabeth and the models were to disembark, go to Antigua, and then back to New York, assuming the airports were open. Christy was still running a fever and Flemming had convinced her that she shouldn't try to go back to New York until she felt better. *That* nagged at her. She'd always hated being bossed around by Tone. It made her want to throw things at him. (She never had.) So why was it okay for Flemming to keep her aboard the boat?

"Christy, I think you should lie down again, don't you? That sunblock makeup is so good that you might have some kind of sunstroke and not realize it."

Obediently, Christy got up and made her way carefully down the steps and back into her bunk. "Holler when we get to St. Vincent," she said, "so I can say good-bye." Even as she said it, she knew that Flemming wouldn't wake her until he climbed in beside her.

What was going to happen when they got back to the real world? Could she work with Flemming in the next office, day after day, without losing her mind?

She'd never had an affair with a married man. But she'd lived through several of them with other editors. The anxiety of not knowing when or how or who would end it. Women droning on about the sizes of their lovers' organs, the number of orgasms they could have between noon and two P.M. Would they lose their lovers because of cellulite? Sagging tits? They worried more about their behinds than their relationships.

She was not going to let that happen. Not ever. Flemming wanted her. Didn't he?

If Tone had wanted her, he would have come to the Caribbean with her. It was the thousandth time she'd gone over it in her mind. He'd be here now. She never would have gone to bed with Flemming. But goddammit she'd *wanted* him. Why was it so hard to admit?

She'd talked to other wives who walked up Fifth or Madison, constantly searching for someone to go to bed with. Christy hadn't believed them. Until now.

How was she going to juggle Skeeter and Antonia and Tone...with Flemming? She'd have to stay in New York more. He lived two blocks from her apartment. All she needed was to be discreet. They'd never know.

They'd know.

Horrible Elizabeth had taken those shots of her in Flemming's arms. Juneau could spot an affair at twenty paces.

Jamie Doran would know instantly.

And Tone would know. The kids would find out.

Christy had a sudden attack of pride. She couldn't go through with the affair once they got back to New York. This was it. One more night on the boat and it would be over. Her first obligation was to Tone, the children, her second, to *Allure*. She'd have to fire Flemming. There was no way she could endure him next to her fifty hours a week in addition to all the trips they'd have to go on together.

She wouldn't tell him tonight. She couldn't ruin it for either of them.

TWENTY-THREE

New York

HOW WAS it possible to accumulate so much crap? Didn't Christy *ever* throw anything out?

Tone had been weeding through closets and drawers for hours. He had several large cardboard boxes from the liquor store for books and important papers; the older they were, the less important they got. He'd already filled the two enormous plastic garbage pails he'd borrowed from the super.

A typhus epidemic in Serbia, in 1915, killed 150,000 people. What on earth had made him write *that* down? F. W. Woolworth died on April 8, 1919, leaving a fortune of $67 million. 1924: Marcus Garvy's plan for resettlement of U.S. blacks was rejected by the Liberian government.

Who was using research like this? It certainly didn't have anything to do with facelifts, stretch marks or combination complexions.

If he read it all, he'd be shoveling for weeks. Faster and faster, he began dumping papers, old notebooks, cancelled checks, hate letters from Bette, into lawn bags. Why bother with the trash cans? What he needed was a dumpster, maybe two.

He'd finished two closets and three drawers in the bottom of Christy's secretary when he took a break for a cold beer. Antonia and Skeeter had both pleaded with him not to tear their possessions apart, and had reassured Tone that they would deal with everything after school. That left his own desk and the large Fibber McGee closet off the library.

He grabbed a beer from the fridge...God, how he missed his deli-fridge in the pool house...rang for the handyman to take away the junk. The longer it sat there in bags, the greater would be his temptation to go back and save half of it.

His desk. Antediluvian files. Papers from law school. No school, no library, wanted the collected papers of Anthony Grantland Shaw. In four hours, he'd plowed through the Fifties and Sixties and was half way through the Seventies.

Juneau Lamb and her fruitless search for her missing daughter. He read through the file. Foster parents dead. The girl had disappeared without a trace after her high school graduation. No record of having gone to college.

The couple who'd reared her: H. Davy Webster and his wife, Judith V. Webster. The girl had gone by Webster, too. Christina Webster.

Good grades. Nothing out of the ordinary. Quiet. Not overly friendly. Loved to read. Very independent. Loved horses. Anxious to please but shy, too.

Tone looked up from the notes he'd gathered so many years before. How many millions of runaway, teenage, rural girls would those descriptions fit?

Christina Webster had vanished. But where? Boston? No one had been able to find her there. Had she gotten married? Become a prostitute? An actress? Jumped off a bridge somewhere?

Apparently the junior partner who'd handled the case

212

hadn't found the answers. Nobody even remembered what color eyes the Webster girl had.

They'd located the property, the Websters' headstone, and discovered that their two sons had been killed in Korea.

So the Websters had raised this pretty little dark-haired girl—their grand-niece, apparently—almost from birth through high school, and then the grand-niece had gone up in a puff of smoke.

They'd checked phone books in Philadelphia, New York, Los Angeles, San Francisco and Chicago. There were Websters coming out of the woodwork, none of them the right Webster.

"Well, Juneau Lamb Webster, whatever the hell your name is, I'm closing the case."

Tone dumped the file. Sad. He felt a twinge. How would he feel if he couldn't find Skeeter?

Preposterous. Skeeter was his best friend. He'd always been with him. Juneau didn't even *know* her mysterious daughter.

Poor Juneau. What had she gotten herself into? Why had it taken her twenty years to decide to track down her daughter? He could understand farming her out if she was too young or too poor to care for her but *why* had she let the child get away from her? He shook his head. All the people who desperately wanted children and couldn't have them. Life wasn't fair. But then who ever said it was.

He hummed a few bars of "I'm Crazy 'Cause I'm Crazy Over You." It needed more work, but the basic idea was there. He'd have to nudge it into shape. Christy might like it better than his plastic money song. She hated that one almost as much as "Beverly Hills Babe." Christ, soon she'd *be* Beverly Hills Babe.

Je-sus. Every time he sang one of his songs, he thought

of Jake Witt. Son-of-a-bitch had some nerve passing out in his birthday suit on one of the French antiques.

He had to find another music man, get Jake Witt out of his life. Out. Just like cleaning house. Tone laughed. Everybody should go over acquaintances each spring or fall, and weed out the rotten ones.

"Next," Tone sang out, digging into another mound of old notes. "Hmm. 'Psychologists have learned that people's perception of themselves is much more powerful in determining personality and behavior than the way they actually look.'"

That described Christy to a T. She was strikingly beautiful. Everyone said so. But she felt dowdy. Dumpy. Awkward.

Suddenly it struck Tone as he meandered back to the kitchen for another cold beer. Christy...Christina Webster. Couldn't be. It was insane. The only thing Christy and Christina Webster had in common was their age and maybe that independent nature one of the teachers had mentioned. Avoiding the limelight had never been part of Christy's personality. Anyone who feared center stage could never, ever be a star at *Allure*. Certainly not the elusive Christina Webster.

Still, Tone reasoned, a woman could change a lot in twelve years. *He'd* changed in twelve years. He'd had to start watching his diet. He put down the beer. Exercise more. Get reading glasses. Erections didn't happen that easily.

But had he changed inside? He had more fun now. Or did he? Twelve years ago, things weren't so god-damned complicated or expensive or boring.

What were the odds of Christy's being Juneau Lamb's daughter? A zillion-to-one? That she'd end up working for her own, unknown mother? Higher still. Life wasn't that neat; things didn't tie up that way. But the more he thought about it...the scraps of information Christy had given him about—what the hell were the names of that aunt and uncle who took care of her...the more he thought about it—damn, could it be?

Hadn't he just seen something on TV about twins, separated at birth, sent to foster homes, who, 30 years later, discovered they lived three blocks apart and had both married girls named Janet and had sons called Steve?

Too much beer, Tone, it's getting to your gray cells. Christy and Juneau Lamb looked about as much alike as...as Mount Vernon and the *Petite Trianon*.

He made up his mind: If it *ever* turned out that Christy was Christina Webster, Juneau's daughter, he wasn't going to tell Christy. Or Juneau.

He loved Christy too much. What good would it do to open up all that hurt again?

Juneau had gotten what she deserved. And so had Christy. They already resented each other, were jealous of each other. What possible good could come out of it?

———————————

He heaved another ten pounds of litter into a bag. God, what a bore. No wonder Christy never cleaned anything out. Totally unrewarding. He didn't even have that virtuous feeling that came after he balanced his checkbook.

A wasted day. He liked to have something to amaze him at least once a day. So far, nothing. Wait a minute— "You did learn something, Tone. Hooray."

He hadn't realized that F. W. Woolworth had died on April 8, 1919, leaving a fortune of $67 million. That was something, back then, something now. Even in his percentile.

The doorbell rang.

"I'm Mrs. Percivale," a plump woman said as he opened

the door, "from Apartment Haven. My, what *is* that curious aroma?"

Tone's sense of smell was nonexistent. He sniffed anyway. Ah. "That's *Georgio*."

"Georgio? You mean a person smells like *that?*"

How could he explain that he'd broken a bottle of perfume and tossed some scented candles into the fire because he'd been pissed at his wife for doing her job?

"No, no, it's perfume. Afraid I broke a bottle in the living room the other day." Maybe that would shut her up.

"The other day? Goodness, I certainly want to get some of this *Georgio*. My perfume only lasts a half hour. This *Georgio* is eternal." She followed her large, fishy nose into the living room.

"What a charming home you have, Mr. Shaw. How can you and your wife bear to give it up?" She wandered into the dining room, the library. "I grew up in an apartment exactly like this."

"So did I," Tone answered.

"I'll just look around at the closets, if I may, Mr. Shaw."

"Let the skeletons hang," Tone said under his breath.

Was Skeeter right? Would Christy ask for a divorce if he sold the apartment?

If she did, he'd say no. This was one time when it was going to be a lot easier to say no than yes.

"Mr. Shaw, oh, Mr. Shaw," trilled Mrs. Percivale. "Your telephone is ringing. Shall I get it for you?"

"No, no, thank you." He rushed over to it. Maybe it was Christy. Maybe she was back.

"Mr. Shaw, this is Doctor Abbott, in North Andover."

Shit. Now what?

"Mother? Is it Mother?"

"I'm afraid she isn't feeling at all well. She's been asking for you. She says there's something she forgot to tell you when you spoke yesterday."

"How bad is she, doctor? She was fine yesterday."

"She slipped in the snow and twisted her ankle."

Just like Mother. Calling for him to pop up to North Andover to check her Ace bandage.

"And?"

"And she caught a chill. Sometimes these things are serious in a woman your mother's age, Mr. Shaw. I don't want to alarm you unduly, but we feel that if you possibly can, you should fly up to Boston."

What Sarah-Jane Grantland Shaw wanted she always got.

"OK," he said. "OK, Doctor Abbott."

He hung up the phone and turned to find Mrs. Percivale looking in their refrigerator.

"Mr. Shaw, I don't think you'll have a bit of trouble selling this apartment. What a gem of a place to hang your hat. Don't see how you can move out. Where are you going?"

"North Andover," Tone said absently, as he let her out the door.

Twenty-four

St. Vincent

MAKING LOVE to Flemming Lord was like opening a Christmas present. First, you admired the ribbon as you untied it; then the paper, silvery, exquisite, the box, the tissue, one last barrier between you and the surprise, then the delicious triumph.

Christy stretched. She'd been dreaming. Her headache was gone. She felt her forehead. Cool at last. She sat up slowly. It was dark outside. She switched on the little lamp mounted beside her bunk, and swung her feet onto the floor. The boat was moving ahead steadily, under power.

"Flemming?" she called softly, as she went up the steps.

She was unprepared for the blaze of stars, the glittering evening laid out before her. As she stood on deck, staring in amazement at the stars, Flemming put his arms around her from behind, turned her gently and kissed her.

"The Caribbean has taken charge of us," he whispered. "Think of all the people out there who are making love."

She was going to ask how he knew but she stopped

herself. He knew everything. Everything except that she was never going to see him again once they arrived in New York. She took gloomy pleasure in contemplating their last night together.

"Why else would anyone be here?"

Quickly she changed the subject.

"Where is the divine Elizabeth? The models? *Every-one?*"

"Gone. Back to New York. The captain is in charge. We're under power and should anchor in about a half hour, for dinner. Feel like some more champagne? I seem to be overstocked. It's my first shoot, you know."

"I know. Flemming, there's something we have to talk about." Her mind was made up. If they didn't talk about it she'd lose her mind. Until this moment, she'd been borne along by dreams, but dreams weren't going to be enough. She needed strength; more strength than she'd ever needed in the past.

"I know, Christy, I know. What's going to happen to us? What are we going to do about it? I know what I want to do, and it scares the hell out of me. I'm thirty-six years old and I've never been in love. Can you believe that?"

"Why wouldn't I?"

"Oh, I guess because thirty-six-year-old New Yorkers are supposed to have been in love a dozen times, had broken hearts, had affairs. Because of all those romantic novels I've written—all of them based on fantasy."

"Don't knock fantasy."

"I want to be with you, Christy. Do you understand what that means?"

She wanted to be with him, too. But there was Tone. He didn't deserve to be hurt.

"It's going to be...well, strange, when we get back." He went on. "We'll only be able to talk about part of the trip, out loud, that is."

Christy's eyes began to fill with tears. How many times today? She was glad of the dark, of the noise of the water against the hull of the schooner.

"I know." Her voice choked. She couldn't say any more.

"It's awful for me, too, Christy. Let's have some of that champagne."

"In a minute. I *know* what you must be feeling, my darling, but at least you don't have a wife."

"But I do, Christy."

"What?" Had she heard him correctly? "Why didn't you tell me?"

"There wasn't time."

Wasn't time? It *had* been less than a week. God, it seemed like a year.

"I'm sorry, Christy."

"Oh, Flemming, it doesn't make any difference. *Yes, it does,*" she added hastily. "It makes it easier."

"Easier? *Easier?*"

"Easier for me to say good-bye. Until now, this minute, I wasn't sure I was going to have the courage. I'm glad you didn't tell me before."

"I couldn't bring myself to tell you. It was all so...incredible, Christy. I—well, I've just never met anyone like you. That's it."

"I've given Tone a hard time, Flemming. A terribly hard time. It wasn't fair."

"Is it fair for him to make you fly to California every weekend?"

"He doesn't *make* me do anything, Flemming. Any more than I make him do things. Can you understand that?"

"I'm not sure. My...wife...April is so different from you. Our life together was nothing like yours and Tone's. Far less complicated."

"Where is April?"

"Yale Law School. She lives in New Haven."

"And what will happen when she's no longer in law school?"

"We haven't faced that yet."

"Oh."

"If it's any comfort, we never had, in six years, what you and I have had these six days."

In a way, that was true for her. But it wasn't enough.

She took both of his hands. "Try to understand, Flemming: Tone is the way he is because I am the way I am."

"OK."

"We're both headstrong, we want our own way. The only way we can stay together is to live apart."

"You're sure he feels this way?"

"Pretty sure. Why else would he insist on keeping that absurd house on Rodeo Drive?"

"Maybe he likes California? It could be that simple."

"Deeper than that, much deeper."

"Tell me, Christy." Whatever it is, maybe she could unblock it with him. In bed she'd given all of herself to him. But there was something in her heart that she kept locked away.

"Flemming, betraying Tone just isn't the answer. I still love him."

"Have you betrayed him, Christy, or, has your heart betrayed you?"

That sounded like something out of one of his novels. But it was true. She shouldn't have trusted her heart.

They sat together for a long time, kissing and watching the stars, trying to find a way to say good-bye.

Suddenly Flemming stood up.

"Time for champagne." In two strides he was at the ice cooler. "Which star shall I aim at?" he asked, beginning to work the cork loose.

"I don't want you to put out the stars, I want you to make them stay there forever, just as they are."

Tomorrow. Antigua. New York. *Allure.* Juneau. The shots. The story on "Age Before Beauty." Tone. Antonia. Skeeter. Cold. Gray. Wet. Slippery.

"Tomorrow, it will all be over."

"But we'll never be over, Christy."

The more they said, the harder it was going to be in the morning. "It's only been a few days, Flemming. We can't be in love."

"But we are."

She ached to tell him how much she loved him, but she held it back, just as she had held so many other things back for most of her life.

"How about some cold lamb? A salad?"

"Can't eat a thing."

"More champagne?"

"Sure."

She was getting sleepy. She started down the steps to her cabin, Flemming behind her.

"I love you, Christy."

Their clothes fell away and they drifted into sleep as calm as the sea.

TWENTY-FIVE

North Andover

SARAH-JANE GRANTLAND Shaw sighed.

"Of course I'm dying, Anthony. We're all dying. Even in Beverly Hills."

"Mother, no one has ever died from a sprained ankle."

"Complications, Anthony, complications. Hand me one of those." She pointed at a dark green glass bottle with a silver top. "Do you understand pain, Tony, dear?"

He had no interest in understanding, thinking about or even discussing pain.

"Mother, why did you want me to come up here?"

"Because I wanted to talk to you and the telephone is too expensive."

So are plane tickets and rental cars from Boston.

"So? Talk."

"You never answer my letters. The thank-you note you claim to have sent regarding that lovely robe has yet to arrive and I suspect that it never will."

"It's the mail, Mother. The mail isn't what it used to be."

"That's true, Anthony. It used to take two months to get a letter from London; it now takes four days. But that's not the point. The point is that I have no idea what you're doing. My own son. I was going to come down to New York when I fell on the damned ice."

"I'm working in Beverly Hills. You know that."

"Are you practicing law?" Her tone was getting more and more imperious. She loved being in charge of a conversation, anybody's.

"Yes. In a way. A type of law."

"That is not an answer."

"I'm a show biz lawyer, Mother. I do contracts. I also produce TV shows and I write songs."

"I believe I heard one of them. 'Beverly Hills Babe.'" She spat the words out. "'I wanna go crusin' with you' I think was what issued forth from my radio. The maid had changed it from my usual station. When they announced the...label...and who 'did' it, I phoned the station to make sure I wasn't hearing things. Anthony, you're a disgrace to 36 Andover Street. Your great-great-grandfather built this house in 1804, and surely you must be the biggest black sheep that's ever set foot in it." She lay back in her pillows, exhausted.

"What about Francis Nelson Grantland and his illegal still? Uncle Tom Grantland, with his two wives? And Mother, don't forget Great-Aunt Catherine Dunne Grantland and the school teacher. And Dad. Dear old Dad. He didn't draw a sober breath for the last forty years of his life."

"Your father, Tony, dear, was a social drinker. But the issue here isn't social drinking. What I'm concerned about is the way you're wasting your mind."

Wasting his...?

"The kind of law you're involved with is thoroughly nitwitted. Those people don't need attorneys, they need video cassettes."

"Mother, would you like some tea?" That way he could get himself a big slug of Scotch.

"Don't patronize me, Anthony. I know you can't stand me. I also know that a boy's best friend is not his mother— it's his wife." She paused. "Now, Anthony, you've had two wives and I'm told you're botching up your second marriage just as badly as you did your first."

How in hell had Mother found out anything about that?

"Mother, you don't know what you're talking about. You don't even speak to Christy. You hardly speak to me."

"Well, I am now, and you'd better listen. Tell your wife to stop going away without you. Move back to New York. Rejoin a law firm. A *decent* law firm before none of them will have you."

"Mother, I've decided to sell the apartment. You know that. I told you. Yesterday."

"I think it's a mistake."

"Since when?"

"Since Skeeter called me."

"Skeeter?"

"He keeps me well-informed. And I think he's right about Christy. If you push her, she'll leave you, and I wouldn't blame her one bit."

"I thought you were against divorce. You sure threw the book at me when Bette and I were divorced."

"That's because I knew how much money it was going to cost you."

"Mother." Tone was genuinely shocked. "I never knew you were so...mercenary."

"There's plenty you don't know, Anthony. Why do you think I really stayed with your father all those terrible years? All that social drinking?"

"I don't know. I assume you loved him."

"Oh, I did. Once. But he became impossible. It was like being married to a talking mummy." She reached

227

for a small glass of brown liquid. "For coughs," she explained.

"What is it? My cough syrup is green."

"Chivas Regal. I stayed, Tony, because I didn't have any money of my own and if I left, your father's mother wouldn't have let him give me any."

Tone was flabbergasted. How well they'd hidden all this nastiness from him.

"Without money, dear, life's decisions are presorted and cancelled for you."

Was this Sarah-Jane Grantland Shaw, making sense for the first time in her life? Maybe she always had and he just hadn't noticed.

"And Anthony, I want to add one thing: You and I are tarred with the same stick. We've always got to be right, have the last word, *win*. Sometimes, we win more if we pretend to lose a little."

"But, Mother, I *have* to win. I can't live with myself if I lose."

"I said *pretend* to lose, Anthony."

He crossed to the bed and took her into his arms. "You know what, Mother? You may be the nicest mother on earth."

"I am. That's why I'm leaving you this house, my antiques and all my money. It's a Shaw house and I want it to continue to be a Shaw house. There's only one stipulation."

"What's that?"

"That you live here."

"Oh." His face fell. But she was only seventy-three. Most of the Grantlands lived to their late nineties. He was safe for a while, at least.

"Don't worry, Tony, I certainly don't want you living here until I'm gone. Frankly I don't blame your wives. I don't see how *any*body can live with you."

He kissed her good-bye, walked down the stairs past generations of Grantlands and Shaws, into the front hall and out into the clear, cold, bright night. He crossed the street to the village common and turned to look at the house. It was hard to believe that it had been there before Hallmark Cards created it. There was a small, twinkling light in each of the eight windows. Smoke curled from the large center chimney. A holly wreath still hung in the center of the fan-lit front door.

He blinked and looked again. Mother was *standing* in the upstairs center window, smiling and waving.

Twenty-six

New York

"I'M REELING, simply reeling," Juneau Lamb marveled, as she went through the pictures Elizabeth had taken on location in Nevis, and on the schooner.

At first, Juneau had been furious. No one deserved to look as good as Christy did in those photographs. It wasn't fair. But, well—what the hell. Why bother getting in a snit over it? After all, what was best for *Allure* was best for her.

"Reed, darling, just look at Christy Shaw. Why, she photographs even better than she looks in real life. Look at the color. Look at her skin. Utterly magnificent. Those models are pigs in pokes next to her. And now for the really knock-out news, Reed. Guess what?"

"I give up." The shots were great, but he was tired. Couldn't this keep until tomorrow? He wanted to take Juneau home and go back to bed. God only knew what would happen after surgery and he was determined to get in as many romantic evenings as possible before it all came to a disappointing, inglorious halt.

"Elizabeth showed the photographs to her current flame who just happens to be a Hollywood producer. The guy is hot for Christy. Suppose something comes of it? What'll we do?"

"We'll have to learn to stop meddling in other people's lives, darling. Simple as that."

"Reed. I can't believe you said that. I mean, Reed, dearest," her voice softened, "we have to keep Christy at the helm of *Allure*."

"She doesn't even know she's going to be at the helm of *Allure*, yet. Remember?"

"Oh, bat burgers! I forgot about that. Where the hell *is* Christy? No call, no telegram, no nothing. Elizabeth is here in New York, why isn't Christy?"

"What did Elizabeth have to say?"

"Only that she wanted to get back with the film as soon as possible. Get them out of the can and into the soup. Does that make any sense to you?"

"My darling Juneau, the only thing that makes any sense to me at the moment is a drink."

"Aha! Here's your answer." Juneau thrust one of the sheets under his nose. "Look."

He studied it. There were several shots of Christy in Flemming Lord's arms. She looked the way he had felt when Juneau had told him about the baby.

"Hmmm. I see what you mean. They certainly seemed to be wrapped up in each other, no pun intended. But please, Juneau. It's seven o'clock, I'm starving and, as Mae West once said, 'I'm ready for a little Scotch and sofa.' Can't we get some dinner?"

"I wish you'd do me a favor, darling, and drop that figure of speech right on its head."

Juneau slipped into her Russian Crown Sable coat. Damn. The Hermes scarf was stuck in the sleeve.

As they walked out of the apartment, her head snuggled against his Irish tweed overcoat, neither of them heard the phone ringing.

———————

"What?" shouted Skeeter Shaw into the telephone. "I can't hear you. Can you talk louder?"

There was a lot of buzzing and crackling on the line. It had to be Christy.

"Who?" More crackling. He couldn't understand West Indian accents. Even on those dumb Calypso records. "Mon, I *hear* your voice, but I don't... I do not understand what you are telling me."

Something had happened. That much Skeeter could figure out. But what?

Statia? Saba? He'd never heard of those places. Maybe he should have paid more attention in geography class. He'd been too busy making bombs, running away, doing homework for other kids, and getting caught. Bar-what? Oh, Bar*buda*. Yes, he understood that the call was coming from the West Indies. Yes, Leeward Islands. He knew where they were. Did he know where Grenada was? St. Vincent? Young Island? His mother was on Young Island? Why couldn't she come to the telephone?

Oh. Something was wrong with the telephone? Tell me about it, mon, Skeeter thought.

"May I speak to Mrs. Shaw?" he shouted into the phone. "That's right. Mrs. Shaw."

The line fizzled out.

"Christy? Christy," Skeeter shouted into the telephone. "Operator? Operator? Shit. Is there anyone there?"

He banged down the phone, picked it up again and dialed the operator. "Operator, I was just talking to the West Indies and I was cut off."

"Where in the West Indies?"

"Young Island."

"Who on Young Island do you want to speak to?"

"Oh, Christ, forget it." Skeeter hung up. There was

233

a time when Thomas Alva Edison had been one of Skeeter's heroes. Not anymore. Teddy Roosevelt was still up there, though. What the fuck would Teddy do in a situation like this?

TWENTY-SEVEN

Somewhere in the Caribbean

A HOWLING squall ripped through the islands, churning up five-foot waves, swallowing small boats, slicing palm trees to shreds.

Christy slept, thanks to a couple of Flemming's valiums. But it was a fitful sleep. She tossed and turned, as though the storm had somehow managed to get inside her body.

Flemming had tried everything. Cool washcloths. An ice bag. Holding her right in his arms. Nothing calmed her. Flemming tucked her in and went above.

What had gotten her into the affair with Flemming? Not just sex. Companionship. Communication. The things she used to have with Tone.

When she'd first married Tone, before she'd made it at *Allure,* they'd had time to be crazy. They'd taken bubble baths together. Licked whipped cream off each other's stomachs. Giggled and laughed. Now, the only time they had any real fun was when they took vacations together. And Tone wouldn't even do that.

Was she trying to turn Flemming into Tone?

She couldn't lie still. She was sinking. Wet. She couldn't get her breath.

g engaged her whole self, gave her energy.
ed her. Sometimes, even, bored her with his
k, his endless neediness.
nely. Desperate to be held. Not just fucked.
Her erogenous zone had become her heart.

That was it! The affair had been building in her head
for...months? Years? Waiting for the right person to
come along...

Flemming. With his sparkling conversation, his sweet
wonderful lovemaking, his gentle, caring gazes.

She was sinking. Water was closing over her head.
Her arms thrashed wildly. She couldn't swim. Where
was Flemming? Where was the captain and his young
assistant? She was drowning.

Water poured over her. She kicked out. Her foot
struck something hard. Pain. She was so fuzzy from the
valiums. Why had she let Flemming talk her into taking
them?

Goddamn Caribbean. She should be home in her bed.
She tried to scream. Nothing.

She'd never see Antonia again. Skeeter. Tone. And
...Flemming. "Help," she screamed, but no sound es-
caped. Her head went under again.

This was her punishment for all that exquisite love-
making. If I ever get out of this, I'll never go to bed
with anyone but Tone. Please, dear God. I promise.
Promise.

I've gotten almost everything I've ever wanted out of
life—a beautiful daughter, an insane great step-son, and
Tone. *Tone.*

Her tears mingled with the sea as a huge and pun-
ishing wave threw her body onto the sand.

It wasn't sand. It was carpet. She was lying on the
floor. The boat had stopped rocking. Moonlight streamed
in through her portholes. Flemming was helping her
up.

236

"Flemming, what…"

"Hush, my darling. You've had a dream. A nightmare, I guess. I couldn't calm you down so I left you alone and went up for a few minutes. You threw yourself out of bed."

"But…but I was in the sea."

"No you weren't. You were in bed the whole time."

"But I'm wet."

"We went through a squall. Some rain came in. See? The sheet is soaked. You're sweating. Too much sun." He drew her into his arms.

A dream. The first dream she could remember without Spirit. She leaned heavily against Flemming, her head beginning to clear. A dream. What had it been about?

Tone and Flemming? No. Her. It had been about *her*.

———

Christy snuggled in the dry, cool, cotton sheets. At last, everything was falling into place. Risking one's life for a bronzer was dumb…*dumb*.

What were her problems, really? Tone was strong-willed. So was she. It was a universal dilemma, the only difference being that most people slugged it out in one place, on Main or Elm Street. She and Tone needed two coasts to slug it out.

It was no longer a question of who won, who was right, who was wrong. Now all that mattered was finding out what was right for both of them…*together*.

But why had she wanted Flemming Lord so much? Maybe what she really wanted was something of her own.

Is that why she'd had Antonia? No. Antonia was a person. Not an answer to Christy's insecurities.

Well, older sure as hell wasn't necessarily wiser. Skeeter had taught her that without even meaning to.

Skeeter. He was the one, the only, person she wanted to talk to right now. With Skeeter, she didn't have to explain. Not anything. Her spirit and Skeeter's, with all of his kid crap, were one. Christy was probably the only prematurely middle-aged woman in America who felt that a sixteen-going-on-seventeenager had a clue as to what it was all about.

He was the link to her world, too. Skeeter could get through to Tone. Tone's mother. Even Antonia trusted him.

Where was the storm? Where was Flemming? It was all a dream and Flemming had become part of the dream...just like Spirit.

Christy turned her sunburned face into the cool pillow to muffle her dry, uncontrollable sobs. Even if she could erase Flemming from her mind, she wouldn't be any happier. The day she forgot him would be the most terrible day of her life.

She stood up and walked to the door. She had to call. Find Skeeter. Tone. She was exhausted. Why did everything always have to happen at once? There was no good time for a meeting or for getting the house painted or for making love. But Flemming had changed all that. With him, any time was the right time. Now, she was never going to see him again.

She opened her door and walked slowly to find the Captain and the short wave radio.

She asked a handsome, young crew member to call New York for her. He said he'd try. It seemed to take hours. Finally, she gave up and went back to bed.

She thought she'd heard Skeeter's voice on the phone. But she wasn't sure.

The story of her life.

What *was* the story of her life? If anyone ever tried to write it, he'd give up in confusion or boredom or both.

238

Flemming had become a part of her soul.

Even *if* she divorced Tone, he divorced the law student, the kids liked him, tolerated him, even *if...* it wouldn't change her life.

Tone's roots were in North Andover, Massachusetts; hers were in the Centurion Building, at *Allure*. One day, Juneau would step aside, leaving her in charge. Christy Shaw. Editor-in-chief.

She reached across the bunk and drew Flemming into her arms. She took him in. He was here. She was here. Tone was somewhere else. But she couldn't go on. It had all been fun. A fling. For some women it was a way of life. Not her. She couldn't juggle Tone and Flemming, Antonia and Skeeter, *Allure,* Juneau and Reed. She didn't want to.

She loved Flemming. She loved Tone. But she loved herself, too.

All at once, Christy knew exactly what she had to do.

TWENTY-EIGHT

All Aboard

IAN LEANED back in his deck chair and sighed.

"Why did you *really* want to go to Tone's birthday party, Bette?"

"I love parties, Ian. You should know that about me by now. And Tone always has smash-eroos." Bette sipped at her rum punch and gazed out to sea. "This cruise was a fab idea, Ian, darling. I think we both needed a little unwinding after that airport mess."

The cruise hadn't been anyone's idea. Bette had won the tickets from a hapless patient with a shattered knee-cap at George Washington University Hospital.

Ian smiled. Bette could make herself believe anything. They were exactly alike.

"*I* think you wanted to see Skeeter."

"Darling, Tone and I have joint custody. I can see Skeeter whenever I wish."

Bette hadn't give a damn about joint or any other custody. She'd pleaded that her international career was so unpredictable that she couldn't adhere to any kind of custody schedule. It gave her a great excuse to drop out of the sky and into Tone's lap whenever the spirit moved her.

"Ah-ha. You just wanted to see Tone's house on Rodeo."

"Darling, I've seen Tone's house. Awful. The living room alone is the gilt-trip of the decade."

Ian smiled. At least Bette was amusing. And she must earn plenty with all those backgammon tournaments. She also had great legs, and excellent taste in restaurants. What more did a man need?

"Bette, know what?"

"Hmmm?"

"You and I deserve each other."

"Where's the news in that? I've known it since we had lunch at Wilton's. Yves Saint Laurent preserve us, do you realize that that was only last week?"

"I know. Seems like we've known each other for the proverbial years, doesn't it? Well, darling, will you marry me?"

For the first time in forty years Bette blushed. "Why, Ian, love." She took him into her arms. "I think I'd like that."

"Well, isn't this great, Bette? Just great. We're both so lonely..."

Bette had never been lonely in her life. Any free time had been spent scheming and plotting to get her own way. She'd been miserable at not being able to wallow in instant gratification. Frustrated at not being able to bend the wills of others to her own. Mad as hell when she'd lost a backgammon game, even a small one. But *lonely*? It was like love. She had no idea what it meant.

"We do get along, Ian, a hell of a lot better than I ever got along with Tone. Of course, there's really nothing wrong with Tone. Nothing that rowing a galley for ten years wouldn't cure. He doesn't know the meaning of the word humility."

He kissed her. "Let's order some champagne to celebrate, shall we?"

242

Ian couldn't wait to send telegrams. The first would go to his ex-wife, Jill, that selfish, arrogant, no-talent bitch. How she had conned that asshole advertising agency into hiring her much less paying her $100 thou a year, was beyond him. What did she need that kind of money for? Especially when she had the income from his grandmother's estate. *His* grandmother's. His stomach started pumping acid. He'd love to see her face when she found out he was marrying *the* Bette Farmington, of London and Palm Beach, international hostess and backgammon champion.

"In just a moment, *mi amore*. We need to talk. Work out a few details in the, shall we say, fuzzy areas?"

Ian leaned back in his chair. "OK. I get $50,000 a year from my ex-wife, provided that I am gainfully employed. I am gainfully employed. So gainfully, that it's pushed up my income tax."

"It can't do that, Ian. No one is in a higher bracket than fifty percent. Don't you know *that?*"

"I didn't. Must have been too busy with my company."

"And what, my love *is* your company?"

"Inflatable Art. Blow-up statues, busts, torsos. Don't laugh, Bette. I started the thing as tax shelter. It's caught on. It's turning into a fucking success."

"I don't believe it."

"Our best seller is King Tut, with Nefertiti a close second. Then, Queen Victoria—that's a bust in a murky bronze shade."

"That's art?" Bette choked. God it was something Tone might have thought of. Maybe Tone and Ian weren't that different after all. They were both crazy. Unpredictable. Geniuses. Well, better than plodding dullards.

"There is no limit, darling Bette, when one is hawking bad taste."

Well, at least Ian made her laugh; Tone had always been too busy talking about how great he was. Anyone with an ego bigger than a gnat couldn't possibly co-exist with Tone.

"OK, darling. I get $80 thou a year from Tone, all of which ceases the instant I remarry, so if you think you're marrying me for my money, forget it."

"I won't renege," Ian said slowly.

"Good, darling, because I think you're right. We *do* deserve each other. Now, let's have that champagne, shall we?"

Ian's stomach felt as though he'd eaten a cement soufflé.

Bette sighed contentedly.

Ian was so intriguing. Definitely nicer than Tone. More fun. And world's apart in bed. His Inflatable Art sounded curious. She'd have her lawyer check it out. And then one day, when they were playing backgammon...who knew what might happen?

TWENTY-NINE

72nd Street

WHAT HAD Flemming said to her? "The difference between a fling and eternal love was that the fling lasts longer"?

Oh, well, if Flemming had misquoted Oscar Wilde, she was sure Oscar wouldn't mind.

She sat huddled at her desk in the library, rereading Tone's letter. He thought he should sell the apartment. The bastard. He thought he should sell Rodeo Drive. Fine with her. His mother was giving him her house in North Andover, and he didn't suppose Christy would like to live in New England? Christy *had* lived in New England, thank you very much. What was he trying to tell her?

She should call him. It was only nine in the evening in California. No, don't call him, dummy. He'll only interrupt and won't remember anything you say.

She rubbed her eyes. What a week. It had seemed more like six months. What had she read in the papers before the trip to L.A.? Something like we're exposed to more messages, more noise, more facts to assimilate, on one day than our grandparents were exposed to in their entire lives?

She'd better not tell Tone that, or he'd have his bags packed for North Andover, Massachusetts, in ten minutes.

Christy smiled as she rolled a sheet of paper into her typewriter. OK, Tone, here goes.

"Dearest Tone," she began, "I'm writing to you, something I've never done before, because for once in my life, I'm not going to give you a chance to break into my train of thought."

Like waving a red flag, Christy thought. Oh, well, no time to falter.

"I see from your letter that you're pissed at me. I wish you weren't. I love you, Tone. I think you know that, but just in case you forgot, I thought I'd remind you.

"We've done plenty of counter-productive things in our lives...to each other...but I still love you. Believe me, I discovered it on my trip to the Caribbean.

"I know how important your career is to you. What you do is far more exciting to you than your marriage. But the simple truth is: You can't live with anyone else and I know I can't either.

"If only...the two worst words in the English language...if only we could both stop trying to win—there's nothing *to* win, Tone—we'd have a lot more fun.

"I have an idea. It's an approach that I worked out on the plane from Antigua.

"Let's put our marriage on a business level, just for the sake of argument."

Oh, Lord, maybe she shouldn't use words like "argument."

"Let's pretend that our marriage is a corporation. We've both worked for it, long and hard. We've both put in countless hours, endured heartbreak, happiness, rewards.

246

"Well, Tone, I've had another offer.

"I won't say a better offer, because I think I really want to stay with our corporation. But a counter-offer. And, much to my surprise and I'm sure, by now, yours, I'm considering it."

Flemming would collapse if he ever read *that*.

"So, Tone, what can we do to improve working conditions so that I'm not tempted to take the counter-offer?

"For starters, we can all live together. Oh, I know. You think we live together now. Well, we don't.

"You have one marriage; I have another.

"You can't change; I can but I don't want to. This does not mean that I like things the way they are. The way they are stinks.

"In our corporation, there is NO PRIVACY. On Rodeo, there are constant comings and goings. You can't look out a window without seeing a strange face. Eyes glazed with dope. Bodies encased in two-hundred-dollar exercise suits.

"It must tire you out, too. So we've got to include more leisure time in our corporation.

"And more conversation. There was a time, Tone, when we couldn't stop talking to each other. Now, we have nothing to say."

Where was she going in this letter? It wasn't actually a threat. She just wanted to make it abundantly clear that circumstances were going to have to change or she *would* marry Flemming.

But what then? He'd have to leave *Allure*. He'd write all day at home. She'd come home from *Allure*, whipped. She'd tell him about split nails. He'd tell her about Chaucer.

"And, Tone," she continued to type, "why do a bunch of other people have to come before me? I'm so tired

247

of other people marching through my life. (I know I'm guilty, too.) Demanding equal time. I want to be with *you*.

"So, let's sit down and talk about all of this as soon as you've read my proposal."

Proposal? That sounded ridiculous. The phone was ringing. Who in hell would call her after midnight? She got to it on the sixth ring.

"Darling girl, this is Juneau. I've been calling you every hour since noon. Listen, darling, the photographs are great. Merely sensational. I couldn't believe my eyes. Divine."

"I'm glad you like them, Juneau. But I can't think about them right now. I'm so tired I can hardly hold the phone."

"Well, hold the phone, Christy, because I have more news."

"Yes?"

"It just can't wait until tomorrow morning. You're the new editor-in-chief at *Allure*."

Christy stared at the letter in the typewriter.

"Christy? Christy? Are you still there? Did you hear what I said?"

Juneau turned from the phone.

"Reed, darling, I think she fainted."

"I—I didn't faint, Juneau. It's just...well, it's that everything is happening at once."

"That's life, pussycat, madame editor. I always knew you could do it, darling."

"What about you, Juneau? Where are you going?"

"I'm going to enjoy myself, darling. I'm going to have a baby."

"Baby?" Had she had too much to drink on the plane?

"You're speaking to the new Mrs. Reed Doran...well, almost the new Mrs. Reed Doran."

248

"Oh, Juneau. That's *wonderful*."

"One last thing, Christy. How did you and Flemming Lord get along on the trip?"

"Uh, terrific, Juneau. He was a terrific help. Terrific."

"Oh, good, dear." Juneau sounded disappointed.

"I think we'll have to let him go. He's interesting, but his heart really isn't into beauty. He's a novelist, first and foremost."

"Let him *go*?" Juneau's voice dropped an octave.

"Yes. Tomorrow. Listen, thank you for the promotion. You know how much I've dreamed of being editor-in-chief. I can't pretend. Not with you."

Then why in hell *was* Christy pretending with her? Juneau wondered. She'd picked it up in Christy's voice. Flemming Lord was more than just terrific. A lot more.

"All right, lovey, I'll see you tomorrow. It's going to be a big day." She hung up before Christy had a chance to say anything else.

Slowly, Christy replaced the receiver.

One more big day, and she would quietly commit herself to the closest sanitarium. Forget the letter. She'd finish it in the morning. Christ, it *was* the morning. She dragged out of the desk chair and started toward the bedroom. The bags could wait. A shower could wait. Only sleep couldn't wait.

She heard a key in the lock. Was it Tone?

He burst into the hall. "Christy? Chris? Greetings from the Coast. Willy Loman is here at last."

The letter. The nitwitted letter. She had to tear it up.

"Christy, I'm *home*."

She ran out of the bedroom into his arms. "Tone, you missed some trip," she whispered, her eyes filling with tears.

"I know. Hey hey—what's this with the viselike grip? I know about the photographs. I know about *Allure*. I also know that Juneau sent you down there with that Lord guy, hoping you'd fall for him and stay in New York."

"*What?*"

"She was afraid that you couldn't commute and run *Allure* at the same time."

"What does she think I've been doing for six or seven or how many years it's been?"

"Who cares what she thinks? Or Reed? Or any of them. Get my letter?"

Christy smiled. "Uh-huh."

"Well, I've decided to sell Rodeo Drive."

Was this her Tone talking?

"But—I know how much you love that house. Beverly Hills. All of it."

Gently, he kissed her.

"You know what, Chris? I love you more."

"Me, too," she said softly. God, it was true.

"I'm sorry about not going to the Islands. I'm sorry about a lot of things. And I know how much your promotion means."

"But—"

"Don't interrupt. It seems we can't say more than three words to each other without one of us butting in. It's bad manners. Now, shut up."

Christy smiled. She was too sleepy to say much of anything.

"Rodeo Drive, out. North Andover, in. I grew up in that house. It's part of me. More than my Beverly Hills Italian cowboy outfits. We don't have to *live* there. Maybe a few weekends. My mother wants to give up the house. It's ours."

"So we'll live here, Tone?"

"Well, it's my father's apartment. I couldn't sell it. Besides, where else would we live? In one of the sliver buildings with a three-by-two living room?" He put his arms around her. How strong and safe she felt.

"Tone, let's go to bed. We can talk about everything in the morning."

At last she had a home. And *they* had a life—beyond Elm or Main or even 72nd Street or Rodeo Drive. It was the street in her head, with the man in her heart. She nestled her head in the pillow and slipped into a deep, dreamless sleep.